THE GLENCOE LITERATURE LIBRARY

Tuck Everlasting

and Related Readings

Glencoe
McGraw-Hill

New York, New York   Columbus, Ohio   Woodland Hills, California   Peoria, Illinois

Acknowledgments

Grateful acknowledgment is given authors, publishers, photographers, museums, and agents for permission to reprint the following copyrighted material. Every effort has been made to determine copyright owners. In case of any omissions, the Publisher will be pleased to make suitable acknowledgments in future editions.

Tuck Everlasting by Natalie Babbitt. Copyright © 1975 by Natalie Babbitt. All rights reserved. Published by arrangement with Farrar, Straus & Giroux, Inc.

Ecclesiastes 3:1–8. Extracts from the Authorized Version of the Bible (The King James Bible), the rights in which are vested in the Crown, are reproduced by permission of the Crown's Patentee, Cambridge University Press.

"Fable" by Merrill Moore. Reprinted by permission of Philosophical Library, New York.

Copyright © 1974 by Jane Yolen. "The Weaver of Tomorrow" first appeared in THE GIRL WHO CRIED FLOWERS AND OTHER TALES, published by HarperCollins Children's Books. Reprinted by permission of Curtis Brown, Ltd.

"The Water of Life" from THE COMPLETE GRIMM'S FAIRY TALES by Margaret Hunt and James Stern (translators). Copyright © 1944 by Pantheon Books, Inc. and renewed 1972 by Random House, Inc. Reprinted by permission of Pantheon Books, a division of Random House, Inc.

THE CIRCLE GAME by Joni Mitchell, © 1966 (Renewed) Crazy Crow Music (BMI). All Rights Reserved. WARNER BROS. PUBLICATIONS U.S. INC., Miami, FL 33014. Used by permission.

From VOYAGES AND DISCOVERIES OF THE COMPANIONS OF COLUMBUS by Washington Irving. Copyright © 1956 Frederick Ungar Publishing Co. Reprinted by permission of Continuum Publishing Co.

Cover Art: Christie's Images

Glencoe/McGraw-Hill

A Division of The McGraw·Hill Companies

Send all inquiries to:
Glencoe/McGraw-Hill
8787 Orion Place
Columbus, OH 43240

ISBN 0-02-817996-X
Printed in the United States of America
2 3 4 5 6 7 8 9 026 04 03 02 01 00

Contents

Tuck Everlasting

Continued

Contents *Continued*

Related Readings

Tuck Everlasting

Natalie Babbitt

Prologue

THE FIRST week of August hangs at the very top of summer, the top of the live-long year, like the highest seat of a Ferris wheel when it pauses in its turning. The weeks that come before are only a climb from balmy spring, and those that follow a drop to the chill of autumn, but the first week of August is motionless, and hot. It is curiously silent, too, with blank white dawns and glaring noons, and sunsets smeared with too much color. Often at night there is lightning, but it quivers all alone. There is no thunder, no relieving rain. These are strange and breathless days, the dog days, when people are led to do things they are sure to be sorry for after.

One day at that time, not so very long ago, three things happened and at first there appeared to be no connection between them.

At dawn, Mae Tuck set out on her horse for the wood at the edge of the village of Treegap. She was going there, as she did once every ten years, to meet her two sons, Miles and Jesse.

At noontime, Winnie Foster, whose family owned the Treegap wood, lost her patience at last and decided to think about running away.

And at sunset a stranger appeared at the Fosters' gate. He was looking for someone, but he didn't say who.

No connection, you would agree. But things can come together in strange ways. The wood was at the center, the hub of the wheel. All wheels must have a hub. A Ferris wheel has one, as the sun is the hub of the wheeling calendar. Fixed points they are, and best left undisturbed, for without them, nothing holds together. But sometimes people find this out too late.

Chapter 1

THE ROAD that led to Treegap had been trod out long before by a herd of cows who were, to say the least, relaxed. It wandered along in curves and easy angles, swayed off and up in a pleasant tangent to the top of a small hill, ambled down again between fringes of bee-hung clover, and then cut sidewise across a meadow. Here its edges blurred. It widened and seemed to pause, suggesting tranquil bovine picnics: slow chewing and thoughtful contemplation of the infinite. And then it went on again and came at last to the wood. But on reaching the shadows of the first trees, it veered sharply, swung out in a wide arc as if, for the first time, it had reason to think where it was going, and passed around.

On the other side of the wood, the sense of easiness dissolved. The road no longer belonged to the cows. It became, instead, and rather abruptly, the property of people. And all at once the sun was uncomfortably hot, the dust oppressive, and the meager grass along its edges somewhat ragged and forlorn. On the left stood the first house, a square and solid cottage with a touch-me-not appearance, surrounded by grass cut painfully to the quick and enclosed by a capable iron fence some four feet high which clearly said, "Move on—we don't want *you* here." So the road went humbly by and made its way, past cottages more and more frequent but less and less forbidding, into the village. But the village doesn't matter, except for the jailhouse and the gallows. The first house only is important; the first house; the road, and the wood.

There was something strange about the wood. If the look of the first house suggested that you'd better pass it by, so did the look of the wood, but for quite a different reason. The house was so proud of itself that you wanted to make a lot of noise as you passed, and maybe even throw a rock or two. But the wood had a sleeping, otherworld appearance that made you want to speak in whispers. This, at least, is what the cows must have thought: "Let it keep its peace; *we* won't disturb it."

Whether the people felt that way about the wood or not is difficult to say. There were some, perhaps, who did. But for the most part the people followed the road around the wood because that was the way it led. There was no road *through* the wood. And anyway, for the people there was another reason to leave the wood to itself: it belonged to the Fosters, the owners of the touch-me-not cottage, and was therefore private property in spite of the fact that it lay outside the fence and was perfectly accessible.

The ownership of land is an odd thing when you come to think of it. How deep, after all, can it go? If a person owns a piece of land, does he own it all the way down, in ever narrowing dimensions, till it meets all other pieces at the center of the earth? Or does ownership consist only of a thin crust under which the friendly worms have never heard of trespassing?

In any case, the wood, being on top—except, of course, for its roots—was owned bud and bough by the Fosters in the touch-me-not cottage, and if they never went there, if they never wandered in among the trees, well, that was their affair. Winnie, the only child of the house, never went there, though she sometimes stood inside the fence, carelessly banging a stick against the iron bars, and looked at it. But she had never been curious about it. Nothing ever seems interesting when it belongs to you—only when it doesn't.

And what is interesting, anyway, about a slim few acres of trees? There will be a dimness shot through with bars of sunlight, a great many squirrels and birds, a deep, damp mattress of leaves on the ground, and all the other things just as familiar if not so pleasant— things like spiders, thorns, and grubs.

In the end, however, it was the cows who were responsible for the wood's isolation, and the cows, through some wisdom they were not wise enough to know that they possessed, were very wise indeed. If they had made their road through the wood instead of around it, then the people would have followed the road. The people would have noticed the giant ash tree at the center of the wood, and then, in time, they'd have noticed the little spring bubbling up among its roots in spite of the pebbles piled there to conceal it. And that would have been a disaster so immense that this weary old earth, owned or not to its fiery core, would have trembled on its axis like a beetle on a pin.

Chapter 2

AND, SO, AT DAWN, that day in the first week of August, Mae Tuck woke up and lay for a while beaming at the cobwebs on the ceiling. At last she said aloud, "The boys'll be home tomorrow!"

Mae's husband, on his back beside her, did not stir. He was still asleep, and the melancholy creases that folded his daytime face were smoothed and slack. He snored gently and for a moment the corners of his mouth turned upward in a smile. Tuck almost never smiled except in sleep.

Mae sat up in bed and looked at him tolerantly. "The boys'll be home tomorrow, " she said again, a little more loudly.

Tuck twitched and the smile vanished. He opened his eyes. "Why'd you have to wake me up?" he sighed. "I was having that dream again, the good one where we're all in heaven and never heard of Treegap."

Mae sat there frowning, a great potato of a woman with a round, sensible face and calm brown eyes. "It's no use having that dream." she said. "Nothing's going to change."

"You tell me that every day," said Tuck, turning away from her onto his side. "Anyways, I can't help what I dream."

"Maybe not," said Mae. "But, all the same, you should've got used to things by now."

Tuck groaned. "I'm going back to sleep," he said.

"Not me," said Mae. "I'm going to take the horse and go down to the wood to meet them."

"Meet who?"

"The boys, Tuck! Our sons. I'm going to ride down to meet them."

"Better not do that," said Tuck.

"I know," said Mae, "but I just can't wait to see them. Anyways, it's been ten years since I went to Treegap. No one'll remember me. I'll ride in at sunset, just to the wood. I won't go into the village. But, even if someone did see me, they won't remember. They never did before, now did they?"

"Suit yourself, then" said Tuck into his pillow. " I'm going back to sleep."

Mae Tuck climbed out of bed and began to dress: three petticoats, a rusty brown skirt with one enormous pocket, an old cotton jacket, and a knitted shawl which she pinned across her bosom with a tarnished metal brooch. The sounds of her dressing were so familiar to Tuck that he could say, without opening his eyes, "You don't need that shawl in the middle of the summer."

Mae ignored this observation. Instead, she said, "Will you be all right? We don't get back till late tomorrow."

Tuck rolled over and made a rueful face at her. "What in the world could possibly happen to me?"

"That's so," said Mae. " I keep forgetting."

"*I* don't," said Tuck. "Have a nice time." And in a moment he was asleep again.

Mae sat on the edge of the bed and pulled on a pair of short leather boots so thin and soft with age it was a wonder they held together. Then she stood and took from the washstand beside the bed a little square-shaped object, a music box painted with roses and lilies of the valley. It was the one pretty thing she owned and she never went anywhere without it. Her fingers strayed to the winding key on its bottom, but glancing at the sleeping Tuck, she shook her head, gave the little box a pat, and dropped it into her pocket. Then, last of all, she pulled down over her ears a blue straw hat with a drooping, exhausted brim.

But, before she put on the hat, she brushed her gray-brown hair and wound it into a bun at the back of her neck. She did this quickly and skillfully without a single glance in the mirror. Mae Tuck didn't need a mirror, though she had one propped up on the washstand. She knew very well what she would see in it; her reflection had long since ceased to interest her. For Mae Tuck, and her husband, and Miles and Jesse, too, had all looked the same for eighty-seven years.

Chapter 3

AT NOON of that same day in the first week of August, Winnie Foster sat on the bristly grass just inside the fence and said to the large toad who was squatting a few yards away across the road, "I will, though. You'll see. Maybe even first thing tomorrow, while everyone's asleep."

It was hard to know whether the toad was listening or not. Certainly, Winnie had given it good reason to ignore her. She had come out to the fence, very cross, very near the boiling point on a day that was itself near to boiling, and had noticed the toad at once. It was the only living thing in sight except for a stationary cloud of hysterical gnats suspended in the heat above the road. Winnie had found some pebbles at the base of the fence and, for lack of any other way to show how she felt, had flung one at the toad. It missed altogether, as she'd fully intended it should, but she made a game of it anyway, tossing pebbles at such an angle that they passed through the gnat cloud on their way to the toad. The gnats were too frantic to notice these intrusions, however, and since every pebble missed its final mark, the toad continued to squat and grimace without so much as a twitch. Possibly it felt resentful. Or perhaps it was only asleep. In either case, it gave her not a glance when at last she ran out of pebbles and sat down to tell it her troubles.

"Look here, toad," she said, thrusting her arms through the bars of the fence and plucking at the weeds on the other side. "I don't think I can stand it much longer."

At this moment a window at the front of the cottage was flung open and a thin voice—her grandmother's—piped, "Winifred! Don't sit on that dirty grass. You'll stain your boots and stockings."

And another, firmer voice—her mother's—added, "Come in now, Winnie. Right away. You'll get heat stroke out there on a day like this. And your lunch is ready."

"See?" said Winnie to the toad. "That's just what I mean. It's like that every minute. If I had a sister or a brother, there'd be someone else for them to watch. But, as it is, there's only me. I'm tired of being looked at all the time. I want to be by myself for a change." She leaned her forehead against the bars and after a short silence went on in a thoughtful tone. "I'm not exactly sure what I'd do, you know, but something interesting—something that's all mine. Something that would make some kind of difference in the world. It'd be nice to have a new name, to start with, one that's not all worn out from being called so much. And I might even decide to have a pet. Maybe a big old toad, like you, that I could keep in a nice cage with lots of grass, and . . ."

At this the toad stirred and blinked. It gave a heave of muscles and plopped its heavy mudball of a body a few inches farther away from her.

"I suppose you're right," said Winnie. "Then you'd be just the way I am, now. Why should you have to be cooped up in a cage, too? It'd be better if I could be like you, out in the open and making up my own mind. Do you know they've hardly ever let me out of this yard all by myself? I'll never be able to do anything important if I stay in here like this. I expect I'd better run away." She paused and peered anxiously at the toad to see how it would receive this staggering idea, but it showed no signs of interest. "You think I wouldn't dare, don't you?" she said accusingly. "I will, though. You'll see. Maybe even first thing in the morning, while everyone's still asleep."

"Winnie!" came a firm voice from the window.

"All *right!* I'm coming!" she cried, exasperated, and then added quickly, "I mean, I'll be right there, Mama." She stood up, brushing at her legs where bits of itchy grass clung to her stockings.

The toad, as if it saw that their interview was over, stirred again, bunched up, and bounced itself clumsily off toward the wood. Winnie watched it go. "Hop away, toad," she called after it. "You'll see. Just wait till morning."

Chapter 4

Aт sunset of that same long day, a stranger came strolling up the road from the village and paused at the Fosters' gate. Winnie was once again in the yard, this time intent on catching fireflies, and at first she didn't notice him. But, after a few moments of watching her, he called out, "Good evening!"

He was remarkably tall and narrow, this stranger standing there. His long chin faded off into a thin, apologetic beard, but his suit was a jaunty yellow that seemed to glow a little in the fading light. A black hat dangled from one hand, and as Winnie came toward him, he passed the other through his dry, gray hair, settling it smoothly. "Well, now," he said in a light voice. "Out for fireflies, are you?"

"Yes," said Winnie.

"A lovely thing to do on a summer evening." said the man richly. "A lovely entertainment. I used to do it myself when I was your age. But, of course that was a long, long time ago." He laughed, gesturing in self-deprecation with long, thin fingers. His tall body moved continuously; a foot tapped, a shoulder twitched. And it moved in angles, rather jerkily. But at the same time he had a kind of grace, like a well-handled marionette. Indeed, he seemed almost to hang suspended there in the twilight. But Winnie, though she was half charmed, was suddenly reminded of the stiff black ribbons they had hung on the door of the cottage for her grandfather's funeral. She frowned and looked at the man more closely. But his smile seemed perfectly all right, quite agreeable and friendly.

"Is this your house?" asked the man, folding his arms now and leaning against the gate.

"Yes," said Winnie. "Do you want to see my father?"

"Perhaps. In a bit," said the man. "But I'd like to talk to you first. Have you and your family lived here long?"

"Oh, yes," said Winnie. "We've lived here forever."

"Forever," the man echoed thoughtfully.

It was not a question, but Winnie decided to explain anyway. "Well, not forever, of course, but as long as there've been any people here. My grandmother was born here. She says this was all trees once, just one big forest everywhere around, but it's mostly all cut down now. Except for the wood."

"I see," said the man, pulling at his beard. "So of course you know everyone, and everything that goes on."

"Well, not especially," said Winnie. "At least, I don't. Why?"

The man lifted his eyebrows. "Oh," he said, "I'm looking for someone. A family."

"I don't know anybody much," said Winnie, with a shrug. "But my father might. You could ask him."

"I believe I shall," said the man. "I do believe I shall."

At this moment the cottage door opened, and in the lamp glow that spilled across the grass, Winnie's grandmother appeared. "Winifred? Who are you talking to out there?"

"It's a man, Granny," she called back. "He says he's looking for someone."

"What's that?" said the old woman. She picked up her skirts and came down the path to the gate. "What did you say he wants?"

The man on the other side of the fence bowed slightly. "Good evening, madam," he said. "How delightful to see you looking so fit."

"And why shouldn't I be fit?" she retorted, peering at him through the fading light. His yellow suit seemed to surprise her, and she squinted suspiciously. "We haven't met, that I can recall. Who are you? Who are you looking for?"

The man answered neither of these questions. Instead, he said, "This young lady tells me you've lived here for a long time, so I thought you would probably know everyone who comes and goes."

The old woman shook her head. "I *don't* know everyone," she said, "nor do I want to. And I don't stand outside in the dark discussing such a thing with strangers. Neither does Winifred. So . . ."

And then she paused. For, through the twilight sounds of crickets and sighing trees, a faint, surprising wisp of music came floating to them , and all three turned toward it, toward the wood. It was a tinkling little melody, and in a few moments it stopped.

"My stars!" said Winnie's grandmother, her eyes round. "I do believe it's come again, after all these years!" She pressed her wrinkled hands together, forgetting the man in the yellow suit. "Did you hear that, Winifred? That's it! That's the elf music I told you about. Why, it's been ages since I heard it last. And this is the first time you've *ever* heard it, isn't it? Wait till we tell your father!" And she seized Winnie's hand and turned to go back into the cottage.

"Wait!" said the man at the gate. He had stiffened, and his voice was eager. "You've heard that music before, you say?"

But, before he could get an answer, it began again and they all stopped to listen. This time it tinkled its way faintly through the little melody three times before it faded.

"It sounds like a music box," said Winnie when it was over.

"Nonsense. It's elves!" crowed her grandmother excitedly. And then she said to the man at the gate, "You'll have to excuse us now." She shook the gate latch under his nose, to make sure it was locked, and then, taking Winnie by the hand once more, she marched up the path into the cottage, shutting the door firmly behind her.

But the man in the yellow suit stood tapping his foot in the road for a long time all alone, looking at the wood. The last stains of sunset had melted away, and the twilight died, too, as he stood there, though its remnants clung reluctantly to everything that was pale in color—pebbles, the dusty road, the figure of the man himself—turning them blue and blurry.

Then the moon rose. The man came to himself and sighed. His expression was one of intense satisfaction. He put on his hat, and in the moonlight his long fingers were graceful and very white. Then he turned and disappeared down the shadowy road, and as he went he whistled, very softly, the tinkling little melody from the wood.

Chapter 5

WINNIE WOKE early next morning. The sun was only just opening its own eye on the eastern horizon and the cottage was full of silence. But she realized that sometime during the night she had made up her mind: she would not run away today. "Where would I go, anyway?" she asked herself. "There's nowhere else I really want to be." But in another part of her head, the dark part where her oldest fears were housed, she knew there was another sort of reason for staying at home: she was afraid to go away alone.

It was one thing to talk about being by yourself, doing important things, but quite another when the opportunity arose. The characters in the stories she read always seemed to go off without a thought or care, but in real life—well, the world was a dangerous place. People were always telling her so. And she would not be able to manage without protection. They were always telling her that, too. No one ever said precisely what it was that she would not be able to manage. But she did not need to ask. Her own imagination supplied the horrors.

Still, it was galling, this having to admit she was afraid. And when she remembered the toad, she felt even more disheartened. What if the toad should be out by the fence again today? What if he should laugh at her secretly and think she was a coward?

Well, anyway, she could at least slip out, right now, she decided, and go into the wood. To see if she could discover what had really made the music the night before. That would be something, anyway. She did not allow herself to consider the idea that making a difference in the world might require a bolder venture. She merely told herself consolingly, "Of course, while I'm in the wood, if I decide never to come back, well then, that will be that." She was able to believe in this because she needed to; and believing, was her own true, promising friend once more.

It was another heavy morning, already hot and breathless, but in the wood the air was cooler and smelled agreeably damp. Winnie had been no more than two slow minutes walking timidly under the interlacing branches when she wondered why she had never come here before. "Why, it's nice!" she thought with great surprise.

For the wood was full of light, entirely different from the light she was used to. It was green and amber and alive, quivering in splotches on the padded ground, fanning into sturdy stripes between the tree trunks. There were little flowers she did not recognize, white and palest blue; and endless, tangled vines; and here and there a fallen log, half rotted but soft with patches of sweet green-velvet moss.

And there were creatures everywhere. The air fairly hummed with their daybreak activity: beetles and birds and squirrels and ants, and countless other things unseen, all gentle and self-absorbed and not in the least alarming. There was even, she saw with satisfaction, the toad. It was squatting on a low stump and she might not have noticed it, for it looked more like a mushroom than a living creature sitting there. As she came abreast of it, however, it blinked, and the movement gave it away.

"See?" she exclaimed, "I told you I'd be here first thing in the morning."

The toad blinked again and nodded. Or perhaps it was only swallowing a fly. But then it nudged itself off the edge of the stump and vanished in the underbrush.

"It must have been watching for me," said Winnie to herself, and was very glad she had come.

She wandered for along time, looking at everything, listening to everything, proud to forget the tight, pruned world outside, humming a little now, trying to remember the pattern of the melody she had heard the night before. And then, up ahead, in a place where the light seemed brighter and the ground somewhat more open, something moved.

Winnie stopped abruptly and crouched down. "If it's really elves," she thought, "I can have a look at them." And, though her instinct was to turn and run, she was pleased to discover that her curiosity was stronger. She began to creep forward. She would go just close enough, she told herself. Just close enough to see. And then she would turn and run. But when she came near, up behind a sheltering tree trunk, and peered around it, her mouth dropped open and all thought of running melted away.

There was a clearing directly in front of here, at the center of which an enormous tree thrust up, its thick roots rumpling the ground ten feet around in every direction. Sitting relaxed with his back against the trunk was a boy, almost a man. And he seemed so glorious to Winnie that she lost her heart at once.

He was thin and sunburned, this wonderful boy, with a thick mop of curly brown hair, and he wore his battered trousers and loose, grubby shirt with as much self-assurance as if they were silk and satin. A pair of green suspenders, more decorative than useful, gave the finishing touch, for he was shoeless and there was a twig tucked between the toes of one foot. He waved the twig idly as he sat there, his face turned up to gaze at the branches far above him. The golden morning light seemed to glow all around him, while brighter patches fell, now on his lean, brown hands, now on his hair and face, as the leaves stirred over his head.

Then he rubbed an ear carelessly, yawned, and stretched. Shifting his position, he turned his attention to a little pile of pebbles next to him. As Winnie watched, scarcely breathing, he moved the pile carefully to one side, pebble by pebble. Beneath the pile, the ground was shiny wet. The boy lifted a final stone and Winnie saw a low spurt of water, arching up and returning, like a fountain, into the ground. He bent and put his lips to the spurt, drinking noiselessly, and then he sat up again and drew his shirt sleeve across his mouth. As he did this, he turned his face in her direction—and their eyes met.

For a long moment they looked at each other in silence, the boy with his arm still raised to his mouth. Neither of them moved. At last his arm fell to his side. "You may as well come out," he said, with a frown.

Winnie stood up, embarrassed and, because of that, resentful. "I didn't mean to watch you," she protested as she stepped into the clearing. "I didn't know anyone would be here."

The boy eyed her as she came forward. "What're *you* doing here?" he asked her sternly.

"It's my wood," sad Winnie, surprised by the question. "I can come here whenever I want to. At least, I was never here before, but I *could* have come, any time."

"Oh," said the boy, relaxing a little. "You're one of the Fosters, then."

"I'm Winnie," she said. "Who are you?"

"I'm Jesse Tuck," he answered. "How do." And he put out a hand. Winnie took his hand, staring at him. He was even more beautiful up close. "Do you live nearby?" she managed at last, letting go of his hand reluctantly. "I never saw you before. Do you come here a lot? No one's supposed to. It's our wood." Then she added quickly, "It's all right, though, if *you* come here. I mean, it's all right with *me*."

The boy grinned. "No, I don't live nearby, and no, I don't come here often. Just passing through. And, thanks, I'm glad it's all right with you."

"That's good," said Winnie irrelevantly. She stepped back and sat down primly a short distance from him. "How old are you, anyway?" she asked, squinting at him.

There was a pause. At last he said, "Why do you want to know?"

"I just wondered," said Winnie.

"All right. I'm one hundred and four years old," he told her solemnly.

"No, I mean really," she persisted.

"Well then," he said, "if you must know, I'm seventeen."

"Seventeen?"

"That's right."

"Oh," said Winnie hopelessly. "Seventeen. That's old."

"You have no idea," he agreed with a nod.

Winnie had the feeling he was laughing at her, but decided it was a nice kind of laughing. "Are you married?" she asked next.

This time he laughed out loud. "No, I'm not married. Are you?"

Now it was Winnie's turn to laugh. "Of course not," she said. "I'm only ten. But I'll be eleven pretty soon."

"And *then* you'll get married," he suggested.

Winnie laughed again, her head on one side, admiring him. And then she pointed to the spurt of water. "Is that good to drink?" she asked. "I'm thirsty."

Jesse Tuck's face was instantly serious. "Oh, that. No—no it's not," he said quickly. "You mustn't drink from it. Comes right up from the ground. Probably pretty dirty." And he began to pile the pebbles over it again.

"But *you* drank some," Winnie reminded him.

"Oh. Did you see that?" He looked at her anxiously. "Well, me, I'll drink anything. I mean, I'm used to it. It wouldn't be good for *you*, though."

"Why not?" said Winnie. She stood up. "It's mine, anyway, if it's in the wood. I want some. I'm about dry as dust." And she went to where he sat, and knelt down beside the pile of pebbles.

"Believe me, Winnie Foster," said Jesse, "it would be terrible for you if you drank any of this water. Just terrible, I can't let you."

"Well, I still don't see why not," said Winnie plaintively. "I'm getting thirstier every minute. If it didn't hurt you, it won't hurt me. If my papa was here, he'd let me have some."

"You're not going to tell him about it, are you?" said Jesse. His face had gone very pale under its sunburn. He stood up and put a bare foot firmly on the pile of pebbles. "I knew this would happen sooner or later. *Now* what am I going to do?"

As he said this, there was a crashing sound among the trees and a voice called, "Jesse?"

"Thank goodness!" said Jesse, blowing out his cheeks in relief. "Here comes Ma and Miles. They'll know what to do."

And sure enough, a big, comfortable-looking woman appeared, leading a fat old horse, and at her side was a young man almost as beautiful as Jesse. It was Mae Tuck with her other son, Jesse's older brother. And at once, when she saw the two of them, Jesse with his foot on the pile of pebbles and Winnie on her knees beside him, she seemed to understand. Her hand flew to her bosom, grasping at the old brooch that fastened her shawl, and her face went bleak. "Well, boys," she said, "here it is. The worst is happening at last."

Chapter 6

AFTERWARD, when she thought about it, it seemed to Winnie that the next few minutes were only a blur. First she was kneeling on the ground, insisting on a drink from the spring, and the next thing she knew, she was seized and swung through the air, openmouthed, and found herself straddling the bouncing back of the fat old horse, with Miles and Jesse trotting along on either side, while Mae ran puffing ahead, dragging on the bridle.

Winnie had often been haunted by visions of what it would be like to be kidnapped. But none of her visions had been like this, with her kidnappers just as alarmed as she was herself. She had always pictured a troupe of burly men with long black mustaches who would tumble her into a blanket and bear her off like a sack of potatoes while she pleaded for mercy. But, instead, it was *they*, Mae Tuck and Miles and Jesse, who were pleading.

"Please, child . . . dear, dear child . . . don't you be scared." This was Mae, trying to run and call back over her shoulder at the same time. "We . . . wouldn't harm you . . . for the world."

"If you'd . . . yelled or anything"—this was Jesse—"someone might've heard you and . . . that's too risky."

And Miles said, "We'll explain it . . . soon as we're far enough away."

Winnie herself was speechless. She clung to the saddle and gave herself up to the astonishing fact that, though her heart was pounding and her backbone felt like a pipe full of cold running water, her head was fiercely calm. Disconnected thoughts presented themselves one by one, as if they had been waiting their turn in line. "So this is what it's like to ride a horse—I was going to run away today anyway—what will they say when I'm not there for breakfast—I wish the toad could see me now—that woman is worried about me—Miles is taller than Jesse—I'd better duck if I don't want this next branch to knock me off."

They had come to the edge of the wood now, with no sign of slowing their rapid jog. The road, where it angles across the meadow, was just ahead, dazzling white in the open sunlight. And there, standing on the road, was the man from the night before, the man in the yellow suit, his black hat on his head.

Discovering him, seeing his surprise, and presented at once with choices, Winnie's mind perversely went blank. Instead of crying out for help, she merely goggled at him as they fled past the spot where he stood. Mae Tuck was the only one who spoke, and the most she could offer was: "Teaching our little girl . . . how to ride!" Only then did it come to Winnie that she ought to shout, wave her arms, do *something*. But the man had fallen away behind by that time, and she was afraid to let go of the saddle, afraid to turn around, lest she fall off the horse. In another moment it was too late. They had sped up the hill and down its other side, and the opportunity was lost.

After another few minutes, the road led them to a place where, off to the left, a shallow stream looped near, with willows and sheltering, scrubby bushes. "Stop!" cried Mae. "We'll stop here!" Miles and Jesse grabbed at the horse's harness and he pulled up abruptly, nearly toppling Winnie off over his neck. "Lift the poor child down," Mae gasped, her chest heaving. "We'll go catch our breath by the water and try to put things straight before we go on."

But the explanation, once they had stumbled to the banks of the stream, came hard. Mae seemed embarrassed, and Miles and Jesse fidgeted, glancing at their mother uneasily. No one knew how to begin. For her part, Winnie, now that the running was over, began to comprehend what was happening, and with the comprehension her throat closed and her mouth went dry as paper. This was no vision. This was real. Strangers were taking her away; they might do anything; she might never see her mother again. And then, thinking of her mother, she saw herself as small, weak, and helpless, and she began to cry, suddenly, crushed as much by outrage as by shock.

Mae Tuck's round face wrinkled in dismay. "Dear Lord, don't cry! Please don't cry, child!" she implored. "We're not bad people, truly we're not. We *had* to bring you away—you'll see why in a minute— and we'll take you back just as soon as we can. Tomorrow. I promise."

When Mae said, "Tomorrow," Winnie's sobs turned to wails. Tomorrow! It was like being told she would be kept away forever. She wanted to go home now, at once, rush back to the safety of the fence and her mother's voice from the window. Mae reached out to her, but she twisted away, her hands over her face, and gave herself up to weeping.

"This is awful!" said Jesse. "Can't you do something, Ma? The poor little tad."

"We ought to 've had some better plan than *this*," said Miles.

"That's the truth," said Mae helplessly. "The dear Lord knows there's been time enough to think of one, and it had to happen sooner or later. We been plain bone lucky it hasn't before now. But I never expected it'd be a *child!*" She reached distractedly into the pocket of her skirt and took out the music box, and without thinking, twisted the winding key with trembling fingers.

When the tinkling little melody began, Winnie's sobbing slowed. She stood by the stream, her hands still over her face, and listened. Yes, it was the same music she had heard the night before. Somehow it calmed her. It was like a ribbon tying her to familiar things. She thought, "When I get home, I'll tell Granny it wasn't elf music after all." She wiped her face as well as she could with her wet hands and turned to Mae. "That's the music I heard last night," she managed between recovering snuffles. "When I was out in my yard. My granny said it was elves."

"Dear me, no," said Mae, peering at her hopefully. "It's only my music box. I didn't suppose anyone could hear it." She held it out to Winnie. "Do you want to take a look at it?"

"It's pretty," said Winnie, taking the little box and turning it over in her hands. The winding key was still revolving, but more and more slowly. The melody faltered. Another few widely spaced notes plinked, and then it stopped.

"Wind it up if you want to," said Mae. "Clockwise."

Winnie turned the key. It clicked faintly. And then, after several more turns, the music began to play again, brisk from its fresh winding, and merry. No one who owned a thing like this could be too disagreeable. Winnie examined the painted roses and lilies of the valley, and smiled in spite of herself. "It's pretty," she repeated, handing it back to Mae.

The music box had relaxed them all. Miles dragged a handkerchief from a back pocket and mopped at his face, and Mae sank down heavily on a rock, pulling off the blue straw hat and fanning herself with it.

"Look here, Winnie Foster, " said Jesse. "We're friends, we really are. But you got to help us. Come sit down, and we'll try to tell you why."

Chapter 7

IT WAS the strangest story Winnie had ever heard. She soon suspected they had never told it before, except to each other—that she was their first real audience; for they gathered around her like children at their mother's knee, each trying to claim her attention, and sometimes they all talked at once, and interrupted each other, in their eagerness.

Eighty-seven years before, the Tucks had come from a long way to the east, looking for a place to settle. In those days the wood was not a wood, it was a forest, just as her grandmother had said: a forest that went on and on and on. They had thought they would start a farm, as soon as they came to the end of the trees. But the trees never seemed to end. When they came to the part that was now the wood, and turned from the trail to find a camping place, they happened on the spring. "It was real nice," said Jesse with a sigh. "It looked just the way it does now. A clearing, lots of sunshine, that big tree with all those knobby roots. We stopped and everyone took a drink, even the horse."

"No," said Mae, "the cat didn't drink. That's important."

"Yes," said Miles, "don't leave that out. We all had a drink, except for the cat."

"Well, anyway," Jesse went on, "the water tasted—sort of strange. But we camped there overnight. And Pa carved a T on the tree trunk, to mark where we'd been. And then we went on."

They had come out of the forest at last, many miles to the west, had found a thinly populated valley, had started their farm. "We put up a house for Ma and Pa," said Miles, "and a little shack for Jesse and me. We figured we'd be starting families of our own pretty soon and would want our own houses."

"That was the first time we figured there was something peculiar," said Mae. "Jesse fell out of a tree . . ."

"I was way up in the middle, " Jesse interrupted, "trying to saw off some of the big branches before we cut her down. I lost my balance and I fell . . ."

"He landed plum on his head, " said Mae with a shudder. "We thought for sure he'd broke his neck. But come to find out, it didn't hurt him a bit!"

"Not long after," Miles went on, "some hunters come one day at sunset. The horse was out grazing by some trees and they shot him. Mistook him for a deer, they said. Can you fancy that? But the thing is, they didn't kill him. The bullet went right on through him and didn't hardly even leave a mark."

"Then Pa got snake bite . . ."

"And Jesse ate the poison toadstools . . ."

"And I cut myself," sad Mae. "Remember? Slicing bread."

But it was the passage of time that worried them most. They had worked the farm, settled down, made friends. But after ten years, then twenty, they had to face the fact that there was something terribly wrong. None of them was getting any older.

"I was more'n forty by then," said Miles sadly. "I was married. I had two children. But, from the look of me, I was still twenty-two. My wife, she finally made up her mind I'd sold my soul to the Devil. She left me. She went away and she took the children with her."

"I'm glad *I* never got married," Jesse put in.

"It was the same with our friends," said Mae. "They come to pull back from us. There was talk about witchcraft. Black magic. Well, you can't hardly blame them, but finally we had to leave the farm. We didn't know where to go. We started back the way we come, just wandering. We was like gypsies. When we got this far, it'd changed, of course. A lot of the trees was gone. There was people, and Treegap— it was a new village. The road was here, but in those days it was mostly just a cow path. We went on into what was left of the wood to make a camp, and when we got to the clearing and the tree and the spring, we remembered it from before."

"*It* hadn't changed, no more'n we had," said Miles. "And that was how we found out. Pa'd carved a T on the tree, remember, twenty years before, but the T was just where it'd been when he done it. The tree hadn't grown one whit in all that time. It was exactly the same. And the T he'd carved was as fresh as if it'd just been put there."

Then they had remembered drinking the water. They—and the horse. But not the cat. The cat had lived a long and happy life on the farm, but had died some ten years before. So they decided at last that the source of their changelessness was the spring.

"When we come to that conclusion," Mae went on, "Tuck said—that's my husband, Angus Tuck—he said he had to be sure, once and for all. He took his shotgun and pointed it at hisself the best way he could, and before we could stop him, he pulled the trigger." There was a long pause. Mae's fingers laced together in her lap, twisted with the tension of remembering. At last she said, "The shot knocked him down. Went into his heart. It *had* to, the way he aimed. And right on through him. It scarcely even left a mark. Just like—*you* know—like you shot a bullet through water. And he was just the same as if he'd never done it."

"After that we went sort of crazy," said Jesse, grinning at the memory. "Heck, we was going to live forever. Can you picture what it felt like to find that out?"

"But then we sat down and talked it over . . ." said Miles.

"We're still talking it over," Jesse added.

"And we figured it'd be very bad if everyone knowed about that spring," said Mae. "We begun to see what it would mean." She peered at Winnie. "Do you understand, child? That water—it stops you right where you are. If you'd had a drink of it today, you'd stay a little girl forever. You'd never grow up, not ever."

"We don't know how it works, or even why," said Miles.

"Pa thinks it's something left over from—well, from some other plan for the way the world should be," said Jesse. "Some plan that didn't work out too good. And so everything was changed. Except that the spring was passed over, somehow or other. Maybe he's right. *I* don't know. But you see, Winnie Foster, when I told you before I'm a hundred and four years old, I was telling the truth. But I'm really only seventeen. And, so far as I know, I'll stay seventeen till the end of the world."

Chapter 8

Winnie did not believe in fairy tales. She had never longed for a magic wand, did not expect to marry a prince, and was scornful— most of the time—of her grandmother's elves. So now she sat, mouth open, wide-eyed, not knowing what to make of this extraordinary story. It couldn't—not a bit of it—be true. And yet:

"It feels so fine to tell somebody!" Jesse exploded. "Just think, Winnie Foster, you're the only person in the world, besides us, who knows about it!"

"Hold on now," said Miles cautiously. "Maybe not. There might be a whole lot of others, for all we know, wandering around just like us."

"Maybe. But *we* don't know them," Jesse pointed out. "We've never had anyone but us to talk about it to. Winnie—isn't it peculiar? And kind of wonderful? Just think of all the things we've seen in the world! All the things we're going to see!"

"That kind of talk'll make her want to rush back and drink a gallon of the stuff, " warned Miles. "There's a whole lot more to it than Jesse Tuck's good times, you know."

"Oh, stuff," said Jesse with a shrug. "We might as well enjoy it, long as we can't change it. You don't have to be such a parson all the time."

"I'm not being a parson," said Miles, "I just think you ought to take it more serious."

"Now, boys," said Mae. She was kneeling by the stream, splashing her face and hands with cool water, "Whew! Such weather!" she exclaimed, sitting back on her heels. She unfastened her brooch, took off her shawl, and toweled her dripping face. "Well, child," she said to Winnie, standing up, "now you share our secret. It's a big, dangerous secret. We got to have your help to keep it. I expect you're full of questions, but we can't stay here no longer." She tied the shawl around her waist then, and sighed. "It pains me to think how your ma and pa will worry, but there's just no way around it. We got to take you home with us. That's the plan. Tuck—he'll want to talk it out, make sure you see why you can't tell no one. But we'll bring you back tomorrow. All right?" And all three of them looked at her hopefully.

"All right," said Winnie. For, she decided, there wasn't any choice. She would have to go. They would probably make her go, anyway, no matter what she said. But she felt there was nothing to be afraid of, not really. For they seemed gentle. Gentle and—in a strange way— childlike. They made her feel old. And the way they spoke to her, the way they looked at her, made her feel special. Important. It was a warm, spreading feeling, entirely new. She liked it, and in spite of their story, she liked them, too—especially Jesse.

But it was Miles who took her hand and said, "It's really fine to have you along, even if it's only for a day or two."

Then Jesse gave a great whoop and leapt into the stream, splash-ing mightily. "What'd you bring for breakfast, Ma?" he cried. "We can eat on the way, can't we? I'm starving!"

So, with the sun riding high on in the sky, they started off again, noisy in the August stillness, eating bread and cheese. Jesse sang funny old songs in a loud voice and swung like a monkey from the branches of trees, showing off shamelessly for Winnie, calling to her, "Hey, Winnie Foster, watch me!" and "Look what I can do!"

And Winnie, laughing at him, lost the last of her alarm. They were friends, *her* friends. She was running away after all, but she was not alone. Closing the gate on her oldest fears as she had closed the gate of her own fenced yard, she discovered the wings she'd always wished she had. And all at once she was elated. Where were the ter-rors she'd been told she should expect? She could not recognize them anywhere. The sweet earth opened out its wide four corners to her like the petals of a flower ready to be picked, and it shimmered with light and possibility till she was dizzy with it. Her mother's voice, the feel of home, receded for the moment, and her thoughts turned for-ward. Why, she, too, might live forever in this remarkable world she was only just discovering! The story of the spring—it might be true! So that, when she was not rolling along on the back of the fat old horse—by choice, this time—she ran shouting down the road, her arms flung out, making more noise than anybody.

It was good. So good, in fact, that through it all, not one of them noticed that the man they had passed on the road, the man in the yel-low suit, had crept up to the bushes by the stream and heard it all, the whole fantastic story. Nor did they notice that he was following now, beside the road far behind, his mouth, above the thin, gray beard, turned ever so slightly toward a smile.

Chapter 9

THE AUGUST SUN rolled up, hung at mid-heaven for a blinding hour, and at last wheeled westward before the journey was done. But Winnie was exhausted long before that. Miles carried her some of the way. The tops of her cheeks were bright pink with sunburn, her nose a vivid, comic red, but she had been rescued from a more serious broiling by Mae, who had finally insisted that she wear the blue straw hat. It came down far over her ears and gave her a clownish appearance, but the shade from its brim was so welcome that Winnie put vanity aside and dozed gratefully in Mile's strong arms, her own arms wound around his neck.

The pastures, fields, and scrubby groves they crossed were vigorous with bees, and crickets leapt before them as if each step released a spring and flung them up like pebbles. But everything else was motionless, dry as biscuit, on the brink of burning, hoarding final reservoirs of sap, trying to hold out till the rain returned, and Queen Anne's lace lay dusty on the surface of the meadows like foam on a painted sea.

It was amazing, then, to climb a long hill, to see ahead another hill, and beyond that the deep green of a scattered pine forest, and as you climbed, to feel the air ease and soften. Winnie revived, sniffing, and was able to ride the horse again, perched behind Mae. And to her oft-repeated question, "Are we almost there?" the welcome answer came at last: "Only a few more minutes now."

A wide stand of dark pines rose up, loomed nearer, and suddenly Jesse was crying, "We're home! This is it, Winnie Foster!" And he and Miles raced on and disappeared among the trees. The horse followed, turning onto a rutted path lumpy with roots, and it was as if they had slipped in under a giant colander. The late sun's brilliance could penetrate only in scattered glimmers, and everything was silent and untouched, the ground muffled with moss and sliding needles, the graceful arms of the pines stretched out protectively in every direction. And it was cool, blessedly cool and green. The horse picked his way carefully, and then ahead the path dropped down a steep embankment; and beyond that, Winnie, peering around Mae's bulk, saw a flash of color and a dazzling sparkle. Down the embankment they swayed and there it was, a plain, homely little house, barn-red, and below it the last of the sun flashing on the wrinkled surface of a tiny lake.

"Oh, *look!*" cried Winnie. "Water!"

At the same time, they heard two enormous splashes, two voices roaring with pleasure.

"It don't take 'em more'n a minute to pile into that pond," said Mae, beaming. "Well, you can't blame 'em in heat like this. You can go in, too, if you want."

Then they were at the door of the little house and Tuck was standing there. "Where's the child?" he demanded, for Winnie was hidden behind his wife. "The boys say you brung along a real, honest-to-goodness, natural child!"

"So I did," said Mae, sliding down off the horse, "and here she is."

Winnie's shyness returned at once when she saw the big man with his sad face and baggy trousers, but as he gazed at her, the warm, pleasing feeling spread through her again. For Tuck's head tilted to one side, his eyes went soft, and the gentlest smile in the world displaced the melancholy creases of his cheeks. He reached up to lift her from the horse's back and he said, "There's just no words to tell you how happy I am to see you. It's the finest thing that's happened in . . ." He interrupted himself, setting Winnie on the ground, and turned to Mae. "Does she know?"

"Course she knows," said Mae. "That's why I brung her back. Winnie, here's my husband, Angus Tuck. Tuck, meet Winnie Foster."

"How do, Winnie Foster," said Tuck, shaking Winnie's hand rather solemnly. "Well, then!" He straightened and peered down at her, and Winnie, looking back into his face, saw an expression there that made her feel like an unexpected present, wrapped in pretty paper and tied with ribbons, in spite of Mae's blue hat, which still enveloped her head. "Well, then," Tuck repeated, "seeing you know, I'll go and say this is the finest thing that's happened in—oh—at least eighty years."

Chapter 10

WINNIE had grown up with order. She was used to it. Under the pitiless double assaults of her mother and grandmother, the cottage where she lived was always squeaking clean, mopped and swept and scoured into limp submission. There was no room for carelessness, no putting things off until later. The Foster women had made a fortress out of duty. Within it, they were indomitable. And Winnie was in training.

So she was unprepared for the homely little house beside the pond, unprepared for the gentle eddies of dust, the silver cobwebs, the mouse who lived—and welcome to him!—in a table drawer. There were only three rooms. The kitchen came first, with an open cabinet where dishes were stacked in perilous towers without the least regard for their varying dimensions. There was an enormous black stove, and a metal sink, and every surface, every wall, was piled and strewn and hung with everything imaginable, from onions to lanterns to wooden spoons to washtubs. And in a corner stood Tuck's forgotten shotgun.

The parlor came next, where the furniture, loose and sloping with age, was set about helter-skelter. An ancient green-plush sofa lolled alone in the center, like yet another mossy fallen log, facing a soot-streaked fireplace still deep in last winter's ashes. The table with the drawer that housed the mouse was pushed off, also alone, into a far corner, and three armchairs and an elderly rocker stood about aimlessly, like strangers at a party, ignoring each other.

Beyond this was the bedroom, where a vast and tipsy brass bed took up most of the space, but there was room beside it for the wash-stand with the lonely mirror, and opposite its foot a cavernous oak wardrobe from which leaked the faint smell of camphor.

Up a steep flight of narrow stairs was a dusty loft—"That's where the boys sleep when they're home," Mae explained—and that was all. And yet it was not quite all. For there was everywhere evidence of their activities, Mae's and Tuck's. Her sewing: patches and scraps of bright cloth; half-completed quilts and braided rugs; a bag of cotton batting with wisps of its contents, like snow, drifting into cracks and corners; the arms of the sofa webbed with strands of thread and dangerous with needles. His wood carving: curly shavings furring the floor, and little heaps of splinters and chips; every surface dim with the sawdust of countless sandings; limbs of unassembled dolls and wooden soldiers; a ship model propped on the mouse's table, waiting for its glue to dry; and a stack of wooden bowls, their sides smoothed to velvet, the topmost bowl filled with a jumble of big wooden spoons and forks, like dry, bleached bones. "We make things to sell," said Mae, surveying the mess approvingly.

And still this was not all. For, on the old beamed ceiling of the parlor, streaks of light swam and danced and wavered like a bright mirage, reflected through the windows from the sunlit surface of the pond. There were bowls of daisies everywhere, gay white and yellow. And over everything was the clean, sweet smell of the water and its weeds, the chatter of a swooping kingfisher, the carol and trill of a dozen other kinds of bird, and occasionally the thrilling bass note of an unastonished bullfrog at ease somewhere along the muddy banks.

Into it all came Winnie, eyes wide, and very much amazed. It was a whole new idea to her that people could live in such disarray, but at the same time she was charmed. It was . . . comfortable. Climbing behind Mae up the stairs to see the loft, she thought to herself: "Maybe it's because they think they have forever to clean it up." And this was followed by another thought, far more revolutionary: "Maybe they just don't care!"

"The boys don't be home very much," said Mae as they came up into the half light of the loft. "But when they are, they bed up here. There's plenty of room." The loft was cluttered, too, with all kinds of odds and ends, but there were two mattresses rolled out on the floor, and fresh sheets and blankets were folded almost neatly on each, waiting to be spread.

"Where do they go when they're away?" asked Winnie. "What do they do?"

"Oh," said Mae, "they go different places, do different things. They work at what jobs they can get, try to bring home some of their money. Miles can do carpentering, and he's a pretty fair blacksmith, too. Jesse now, *he* don't ever seem too settled in himself. Course, he's young." She stopped and smiled. "That sounds funny, don't it? Still, it's true, just the same. So Jesse, he does what strikes him at the moment, working in the fields, or in saloons, things like that, whatever he comes across. But they can't stay on in any one place for long, you know. None of us can. People get to wondering." She sighed. "We been in this house about as long as we dare, going on twenty years. It's a right nice place. Tuck's got so's he's real attached to it. Then, too, it's off by itself, plenty of fish in the pond, not too far from the towns around. When we need things, we go sometimes to one, sometimes the next, so people don't come to notice us much. And we sell where we can. But I guess we'll be moving on, one of these days. It's just about time."

It sounded rather sad to Winnie, never to belong anywhere. "That's too bad," she said, glancing shyly at Mae. "Always moving around and never having any friends or anything."

But Mae shrugged off this observation. "Tuck and me, we got each other," she said, "and that's a lot. The boys, now they go their separate ways. They're some different, don't always get on too good. But they come home whenever the spirit moves, and every ten years, first week of August, they meet at the spring and come home *together* so's we can be a family again for a little while. That's why we was there this morning. One way or another, it all works out." She folded her arms and nodded, more to herself than to Winnie. "Life's got to be lived, no matter how long or short," she said calmly. "You got to take what comes. We just go along, like everybody else, one day at a time. Funny—we don't feel no different. Leastwise, I don't. Sometimes I forget about what's happened to us, forget it altogether. And then sometimes it comes over me and I wonder why it happened to *us*. We're plain as salt, us Tucks. We don't deserve no blessings—if it is a blessing. And, likewise, I don't see how we deserve to be cursed, if it's a curse. Still—there's no use trying to figure why things fall the way they do. Things just are, and fussing don't bring changes. Tuck, now, he's got a few other ideas, but I expect he'll tell you. There! The boys are in from the pond."

Winnie heard a burst of voices downstairs, and in a moment Miles and Jesse were climbing to the loft.

"Here child," said Mae hastily. "Hide your eyes. Boys? Are you decent? What'd you put on to swim in? I got Winnie up here, do you hear me?"

"For goodness' sake, Ma," said Jesse, emerging from the stairwell. "You think we're going to march around in our altogether with Winnie Foster in the house?"

And Miles, behind him, said, "We just jumped in with our clothes on. Too hot and tired to shed 'em."

It was true. They stood there side by side with their wet clothes plastered to their skins, little pools of water collecting at their feet.

"Well!" said Mae, relieved. "All right. Find something dry to put on. Your pa's got supper nearly ready." And she hustled Winnie down the narrow stairs.

Chapter 11

IT WAS a good supper, flapjacks, bacon, bread, and applesauce, but they ate sitting about in the parlor instead of around a table. Winnie had never had a meal that way before and she watched them carefully at first, to see what rules there might be that she did not know about. But there seemed to be no rules. Jesse sat on the floor and used the seat of a chair for a table, but the others held their plates in their laps. There were no napkins. It was all right, then, to lick the maple syrup from your fingers. Winnie was never allowed to do such a thing at home, but she had always thought it would be the easiest way. And suddenly the meal seemed luxurious.

After a few minutes, however, it was clear to Winnie that there was at least one rule: As long as there was food to eat, there was no conversation. All four Tucks kept their eyes and their attention on the business at hand. And in the silence, given time to think, Winnie felt her elation, and her thoughtless pleasure, wobble and collapse.

It had been different when they were out-of-doors, where the world belonged to everyone and no one. Here, everything was theirs alone, everything was done their way. Eating, she realized now, was a very personal thing, not something to do with strangers. *Chewing* was a personal thing. Yet here she was, chewing with strangers in a strange place. She shivered a little, and frowned, looking round at them. That story they had told her—why, they were crazy, she thought harshly, and they were criminals. They had kidnapped her, right out of the middle of her very own wood, and now she would be expected to sleep—*all night*—in this dirty, peculiar house. She had never slept in any bed but her own in her life. All these thoughts flowed at once from the dark part of her mind. She put down her fork and said, unsteadily, "I want to go home."

The Tucks stopped eating, and looked at her, surprised. Mae said soothingly, "Why, of course you do, child. That's only natural. I'll take you home. I promised I would, soon's we've explained a bit as to why you got to promise you'll never tell about the spring. That's the only reason we brung you here. We got to make you see why."

Then Miles said, cheerfully and with sudden sympathy, "There's a pretty good old rowboat. I'll take you out for a row after supper."

"No, *I* will," said Jesse. "Let *me*. I found her first, didn't I, Winnie Foster? Listen, I'll show you where the frogs are and . . ."

"Hush," Tuck interrupted. "Everyone hush. *I'll* take Winnie rowing on the pond. There's a good deal to be said and I think we better hurry up and say it. I got a feeling there ain't a whole lot of time."

Jesse laughed at this, and ran a hand roughly through his curls. "That's funny, Pa. Seems to me like time's the only thing we got a lot of."

But Mae frowned. "You worried, Tuck? What's got you? No one saw us on the way up. Well, now, wait a bit—yes, they did, come to think of it. There was a man on the road, just outside Treegap. But he didn't say nothing."

"He knows me, though," said Winnie. She had forgotten, too, about the man in the yellow suit, and now, thinking of him, she felt a surge of relief. "He'll tell my father he saw me."

"He knows you?" said Mae, her frown deepening. "But you didn't call out to him, child. Why not?"

"I was too scared to do *anything*," said Winnie honestly.

Tuck shook his head. "I never thought we'd come to the place where we'd be scaring children." he said. "I guess there's no way to make it up to you, Winnie, but I'm sure most awful sorry it had to happen like that. Who was this man you saw?"

"I don't know his name," said Winnie. "But he's a pretty nice man, I guess." In fact, he seemed supremely nice to her now, a kind of savior. And then she added, "He came to our house last night, but he didn't go inside."

"Well, that don't sound too serious, Pa," said Miles. "Just some stranger passing by."

"Just the same, we got to get you home again, Winnie," said Tuck, standing up decisively. "We got to get you home just as fast as we can. I got a feeling this whole thing is going to come apart like wet bread. But first we got to talk, and the pond's the best place. The pond's got answers. Come along, child. Let's go out on the water."

Chapter 12

THE SKY was a ragged blaze of red and pink and orange, and its double trembled on the surface of the pond like color spilled from a paintbox. The sun was dropping fast now, a soft red sliding egg yolk, and already to the east there was a darkening to purple. Winnie, newly brave with her thoughts of being rescued, climbed boldly into the rowboat. The hard heels of buttoned boots made a hollow banging sound against its wet boards, loud in the warm and breathless quiet. Across the pond a bullfrog spoke a deep note of warning. Tuck climbed in, too, pushing off, settling the oars into their locks, dipped them into the silty bottom in one strong pull. The rowboat slipped from the bank then, silently, and glided out, tall water grasses whispering away from its sides, releasing it.

Here and there the still surface of the water dimpled, and bright rings spread noiselessly and vanished. "Feeding time," said Tuck softly. And Winnie, looking down, saw hosts of tiny insects skittering and skating on the surface. "Best time of all for fishing," he said "when they come up to feed."

He dragged on the oars. The rowboat slowed and began to drift gently toward the farthest end of the pond. It was so quiet that Winnie almost jumped when the bullfrog spoke again. And then, from the tall pines and birches that ringed the pond, a wood thrush caroled. The silver notes were pure and clear and lovely.

"Know what that is, all around us, Winnie?" said Tuck, his voice low. "Life. Moving, growing, changing, never the same two minutes together. This water, you look out at it every morning, and it *looks* the same, but it ain't. All night long it's been moving, coming in through the stream back there to the west, slipping out through the stream down east here, always quiet, always new, moving on. You can't hardly see the current, can you? And sometimes the wind makes it look like it's going the other way. But it's always there, the water's always moving on, and someday, after a long while, it comes to the ocean."

They drifted in silence for a time. The bullfrog spoke again, and from behind them, far back in some reedy, secret place, another bull-frog answered. In the fading light, the trees along the banks were slowly losing their dimensions, flattening into silhouettes clipped from black paper and pasted to the paling sky. The voice of a different frog, hoarser and not so deep, croaked from the nearest bank.

"Know what happens then?" said Tuck. "To the water? The sun sucks some of it up right out of the ocean and carries it back in clouds, and then it rains, and the rain falls into the stream, and the stream keeps moving on, taking it all back again. It's a wheel, Winnie. Everything's a wheel, turning and turning, never stopping. The frogs is part of it, and the bugs, and the fish, and the wood thrush, too. And people, But never the same ones. Always coming in new, always growing and changing, and always moving on. That's the way it's supposed to be. That's the way it *is*."

The rowboat had drifted at last to the end of the pond, but now its bow bumped into the rotting branches of a fallen tree that thrust thick fingers into the water. And though the current pulled at it, dragging its stern sidewise, the boat was wedged and could not follow. The water slipped past it, out between clumps of reeds and brambles and gurgled down a narrow bed, over stones and pebbles, foaming a little, moving swiftly now after its slow trip between the pond's wide banks. And, farther down, Winnie could see that it hurried into a curve, around a leaning willow, and disappeared.

"It goes on," Tuck repeated, "to the ocean. But this rowboat now, it's stuck. If we didn't move it out ourself, it would stay here forever, trying to get loose, but stuck. That's what us Tucks are, Winnie. Stuck so's we can't move on. We ain't part of the wheel no more. Dropped off, Winnie. Left behind. And everywhere around us, things is moving and growing and changing. You, for instance. A child now, but someday a woman. And after that, moving on to make room for the new children."

Winnie blinked, and all at once her mind was drowned with understanding of what he was saying. For she—yes, even she—would go out of the world willy-nilly someday. Just go out, like the flame of a candle, and no use protesting. It was a certainty. She would try very hard not to think of it, but sometimes, as now, it would be forced upon her. She raged against it, helpless and insulted, and blurted at last, "I don't want to die."

"No," said Tuck calmly. "Not now. Your time's not now. But

dying's part of the wheel, right there next to being born. You can't pick the pieces you like and leave the rest. Being part of the whole thing, that's the blessing. But it's passing us by, us Tucks. Living's heavy work, but off to one side, the way *we* are, it's useless, too. It don't make sense. If I knowed how to climb back on the wheel, I'd do it in a minute. You can't have living without dying. So you can't call it living, what we got. We just *are*, we just *be*, like rocks beside the road."

Tuck's voice was rough now, and Winnie, amazed, sat rigid. No one had ever talked to her of things like this before. "I want to grow again," he said fiercely, "and change. And if that means I got to move on at the end of it, then I want that, too. Listen, Winnie, it's something you don't find out how you feel until afterwards. If people knowed about the spring down there in Treegap, they'd all come running like pigs to slops. They'd trample each other, trying to get some of that water. That'd be bad enough, but afterwards—can you imagine? All the little ones little forever, all the old ones old forever. Can you picture what that means? *Forever?* The wheel would keep on going round, the water rolling by to the ocean, but the people would've turned into nothing but rocks by the side of the road. "Cause they wouldn't know till after, and then it'd be too late." He peered at her, and Winnie saw that his face was pinched with the effort of explaining. "Do you see, now, child? Do you understand? Oh, Lord, I just got to make you understand!"

There was a long moment of silence. Winnie, struggling with the anguish of all these things, could only sit hunched and numb, the sound of the water rolling in her ears. It was black and silky now; it lapped at the sides of the rowboat and hurried on around them into the stream.

And then, down the length of the pond, a voice rang out. It was Miles, and every word, across the water, came clearly to their ears. "Pa! Pa, come back! Something's happened, Pa. The horse is gone. Can you hear me? Someone's stole the horse."

Chapter 13

SOMETIME LATER, the man in the yellow suit slipped down from the saddle and tied the Tucks' old horse to a bar of the Fosters' fence. He tried the gate. It was unlocked. He pushed through and strode up the path to the door of the cottage. Though it was late now, almost midnight, the windows glowed golden: the family had not gone to bed. The man in the yellow suit took off his hat and smoothed his hair with long white fingers. Then he knocked at the door. It was opened at once by Winnie's grandmother, and before she could speak, the man said quickly, "Ah! Good evening! May I come in? I have happy news for you. I know where they've taken the little girl."

Chapter 14

THERE HAD BEEN NOTHING for the Tucks to do but go to bed. It was too dark now to go out looking for the horse thief, and anyway, they had no idea when he had done his thieving or which way he had gone.

"That beats all, though, don't it Pa," said Jesse, "coming up to a person's house and stealing their horse right out from under their nose!"

"I got to give you that," said Tuck. "But the question is, was it just some ordinary thief, or was it someone that had some special reason? I don't like it. I got a bad feeling about the whole thing."

"Hush now, Tuck," said Mae. She was spreading a quilt on the old sofa, making it a bed for Winnie. "You're too much of a worrier. There's nothing we can do about it now, so there's no need fussing. You got no reason to think there's anything peculiar about it, anyway. Come on, we'll get a good night's sleep and figure it out in the morning when we're fresh. Boys, up you go, and don't get talking—you'll keep us awake. Winnie, child, you bed down, too. You'll sleep first-rate on the sofa here."

But Winnie did not sleep at all, not for a long, long time. The cushions of the sofa were remarkably lumpy and smelled like old newspapers; and the chair pad Mae had given her for a pillow was thin and hard, and rough under her cheek. But far worse than this was the fact that she was still in her clothes, for she had firmly refused the offer of Mae's spare nightgown, with its seeming miles of faded cotton flannel. Only her own nightgown would do, and the regular bedtime routine; without them, she was painfully lonely for home. Her joy on the road that morning had completely disappeared; the wide world shrank and her older fears rolled freely in her consciousness. It was unbelievable that she should be in this place; it was an outrage. But she was helpless to do anything about it, helpless to control it, and exhausted by the conversation in the rowboat.

Was it true? Could they really never die, these Tucks? It had evidently not occurred to them that she might not believe it. They were only concerned that she keep the secret. Well, she did not believe it. It was nonsense. Wasn't it? Well, wasn't it?

Winnie's head whirled. Remembering the man in the yellow suit was the only thing that kept her from weeping. "He's told them by now," she thought, rehearsing it. "They've been looking for me for hours. But they don't know where to look! No. The man saw which way we were headed. Papa will find me. They're out looking for me right now."

She went over it again and again, lying wrapped in the quilt, while outside the moon rose, turning the pond to silver. There was a hint of mist, now that the air was cooler, and the frogs talked comfortably. Crickets soon joined in with their shrill, rhythmic song. In the table drawer, the mouse rustled softly, enjoying the supper of flapjack crumbs Mae had put there for him. And at last these things were clearer in Winnie's ears than the voice of her thoughts. She began to relax, listening to the sound-filled silence. Then, just as she was drifting into sleep, she heard soft footsteps and Mae was beside her. "You resting easy, child?" she whispered.

"I'm all right, thank you." said Winnie.

"I'm sorry about everything," said Mae. "I just didn't know no other way but to bring you back with us. I know it ain't very happy for you here, but . . . well . . . anyway, you have a good talk with Tuck?"

"I guess so," said Winnie.

"That's good. Well. I'm going back to bed. Get a good sleep."

"All right," said Winnie.

But still Mae lingered. "We been alone so long," she said at last, "I guess we don't know how to do with visitors. But still and all, it's a good feeling, you being here with us. I wish you was . . . ours." She put out an awkward hand then and touched Winnie's hair. "Well," she said, "good night."

"Good night," said Winnie.

Tuck came, too, a little later, to peer down at her anxiously. He was wearing a long white nightshirt and his hair was rumpled. "Oh!" he said. "You still awake? Everything all right?"

"Yes," said Winnie.

"I didn't mean to go disturbing you," he said. "But I been laying in there thinking I ought to be setting out here with you till you went to sleep."

"You don't have to do that," said Winnie, surprised and touched. "I'm all right."

He looked uncertain. "Well . . . but if you want something, will you holler? I'm just in the next room—I'd be out here like a shot." And then he added, gruffly, "It's been quite a time since we had a natural, growing child in the house . . ." His voice trailed off. "Well. Try to get some sleep. That sofa there, I guess it ain't the kind of thing you're used to."

"It's fine," said Winnie.

"The bed's no better, or I'd switch with you," he said. He didn't seem to know how to finish the conversation. But then he bent and kissed her quickly on the cheek, and was gone.

Winnie lay with her eyes wide. She felt cared for and—confused. And all at once she wondered what would happen to the Tucks when her father came. What would he do to them? She would never be able to explain how they had been with her, how they made her feel. She remembered guiltily that at supper she had decided they were criminals. Well, but they *were*. And yet . . .

And then a final visitor made her confusion complete. There was a creaking on the loft stairs and Jesse was looking down at her, very beautiful and eager in the faint blue moonlight. "Hey, Winnie Foster," he whispered. "You asleep?"

This time she sat up, pulling the quilt around her in sudden embarrassment, and answered, "No, not yet."

"Well then, listen." He knelt beside her, his curls tumbled and his eyes wide. "I been thinking it over. Pa's right about you having to keep the secret. It's not hard to see why. But the thing is, you knowing about the water already, and living right next to it so's you could go there any time, well, listen, how'd it be if you was to wait until you're seventeen, same age as me—heck, that's only six years off—and then you could go and drink some, and then you could go away with me! We could get married, even. That'd be pretty good, wouldn't it! We could have a grand old time, go all around the world, see everything. Listen, Ma and Pa and Miles, they don't know how to enjoy it, what we got. Why, heck, Winnie, life's to enjoy yourself, isn't it? What else is it good for? That's what *I* say. And you and me, we could have a good time that never, never stopped. Wouldn't that be something?

Once more Winnie adored him, kneeling there beside her in the moonlight. He wasn't crazy. How could he be? He was just—amazing. But she was struck dumb. All she could do was stare at him.

"You think on it, Winnie Foster," Jesse whispered earnestly. "Think on it some and see if it don't sound good. Anyway, I'll see you in the morning. All right?"

"All right," she managed to whisper in return. He slipped away then, back up the creaking steps, but Winnie sat upright, wide awake, her cheeks burning. She could not deal with this remarkable suggestion, she could not "think on it." For she didn't know what to believe about anything. She lay down again, finally, and stared into the moonlight for another half an hour before she fell asleep.

Chapter 15

IN TREEGAP, the same moonlight silvered the roof of the touch-me-not cottage, but inside, the lamps were burning. "That's right," said the man in the yellow suit. "I know where she is." He sat back in his chair in the Fosters' spotless parlor, crossing his long, thin legs, and the suspended foot began a rhythmic jiggling. He hung his hat on his knee and smiled, his eyes nearly closed. "I followed them, you see. She's with them now. As soon as I saw they'd arrived at their destination, I turned around and came directly back. I thought you'd be staying up. You've been looking for her all day, of course. It must be quite a worry."

He lifted a hand then, ignoring their exclamations, and began to smooth the thin hairs of his beard. "You know," he said thoughtfully, "I've come a long way looking for a wood exactly like the one you've got next door here. It would mean a great deal to me to own it. And how pleasant to have neighbors like yourselves! Now, understand, I wouldn't cut down many of the trees. I'm no barbarian, you can see that. No, just a few. You wouldn't find it different at all, really." He gestured with his long, white fingers and smiled, his face crinkling pleasantly. "We'd be good friends, I think. Why, the little girl and I, we're friends already. It would be a great relief to see her safely home again, wouldn't it?" He clicked his tongue and frowned. "Dreadful thing, kidnapping. Isn't it fortunate that I was a witness! Why, without me, you might never have heard a word. They're rough country people, the ones that took her. There's just no telling what illiterates like that might do. Yes," he sighed, lifting his eyebrows and smiling again, "it looks as if I'm the only person in the whole world who knows where to find her."

And then the man in the yellow suit sat forward. His long face took on a hard expression. "Now, I don't have to spell things out for people like yourselves. Some types one comes across can't seem to cut their way through any problem, and that does make things difficult. But you, I don't have to explain the situation to *you*. I've got what you want, and you've got what I want. Of course, you might find that child without me, but . . . you might not find her in time. So: I want the wood and you want the child. It's a trade. A simple, clear-cut trade."

He looked around at the three shocked faces, and as if he were seeing nothing there but calm agreement, he smiled delightedly and rubbed his hands together. "Done and done," he said, "I knew right away, I said to myself, 'Now here is a group of intelligent, reasonable people!' I'm seldom wrong as a judge of character. Very seldom disappointed. So! All that remains is to write it up on paper, giving me the wood, and to sign it. It's best, don't you agree, to keep things legal and tidy. The rest is easy. Nothing to it. You go for your local constable, and he and I ride out and bring back the child *and* the criminals. No—oh no, Mr. Foster—I understand your concern, but you mustn't come along. We'll do this business my way. There now! Your terrible ordeal is as good as over, isn't it? I'm so thankful I was here to help you out!"

Chapter 16

THE CONSTABLE was fat, and he was sleepy. He wheezed when he spoke. And he spoke quite a bit as they started off, he and the man in the yellow suit. "First they roust me out of bed in the middle of the night, after I been out since sun-up looking for that child, and now I s'pose your going to try to run me all the way," he said sourly. "I got to tell you this horse of mine is none too strong. I don't have to hurry her as a rule, so most of the time it don't matter. Seems to me we could've waited till dawn, anyway."

The man in the yellow suit was a courteous as always. "The Fosters have been waiting since yesterday morning," he pointed out. "Naturally, they're very upset. The sooner we get there, the sooner that child will be with them again."

"How come *you're* so deep in it?" asked the constable suspiciously. "Maybe you're in cahoots with the kidnappers, how do I know? You should of reported it right off, when you saw her snatched."

The man in the yellow suit sighed. "But of course I had to find out where they were taking her," he explained patiently. "I came right back after that. And the Fosters are friends of mine. They've—uh—sold me their wood."

The constable's eyes went round. "I'll be!" he said. "What do you know about that! I didn't suppose they'd ever do a thing like that, friend or no friend. They're the first family around here, you know. Proud as peacocks, all of 'em. Family-proud, and land-proud, too. But they sold off, did they? Well, well," And he whistled in amazement.

They thumped along in silence for a while, out around the wood and across the star-lit meadow. Then the constable yawned deeply and said, "You ready to tell me how long this is going to take? How far we got to go?"

"Twenty miles north," said the man in the yellow suit.

The constable groaned. "Twenty miles!" He shifted the shotgun that rested across his saddle, and groaned again. "Clear up in the foothills? That's a fair way, all right."

There was no reply to this. The constable ran his fingers down the gleaming barrel of the shotgun. Then he shrugged, and slumped a little in the saddle. "Might as well relax," he wheezed, suddenly companionable. "We'll be riding three, four hours."

Still there was no reply.

"Yessir," said the constable, trying again. "It's something new for these parts, kidnapping. Never had a case like this before that I know of, and I been in charge for going on fifteen years."

He waited.

"You don't say so," his companion said at last.

"Yep, that's a fact," said the constable, with evident relief. Maybe now there would be some conversation! "Yep, fifteen years. Seen a lot of trouble in fifteen years, but nothing quite like this. 'Course, there's a first time for everything, as they say. We got a brand-new jailhouse, did you notice? Listen, it's a dandy! Give those folks nice clean accommodations." He chuckled. "'Course, they won't be there long. Circuit judge'll be coming through next week. He'll send 'em over to Charleyville, most likely, to the county jail. That's what they do for your serious crimes. 'Course, we got a gallows of our own, if we ever need it. Keeps down trouble, *I* think, just having it there. Ain't ever used it yet. That's because they take care of the serious stuff over to Charleyville, like I say."

The constable paused to light a cigar, and went on cheerfully: "What you got planned for that piece of Foster land? Going to clear her? Put up a house, or a store, maybe?"

"No," said the man in the yellow suit.

The constable waited for more, but there was no more. His sour mood returned. He frowned and shook the ashes from his cigar. "Say," he said. "you're kind of a close-lipped feller, ain't you?"

The man in the yellow suit narrowed his eyes. His mouth, above the thin gray beard, twitched with annoyance. "Look here," he said tightly. "Would you mind if I rode on ahead? I'm worried about that child. I'll tell you how to get there, and I'll go ahead and keep watch."

"Well," said the constable grudgingly, "all right, if you're in such a ding-danged hurry. But don't do nothing till I get there. Those folks are likely dangerous. I'll try to keep up, but this horse of mine, she's none too strong. Don't see as how I could get her to a gallop, even if I tried."

"That's right," said the man in the yellow suit. "So I'll go on ahead, and wait outside the house till you get there."

He explained the route carefully, then dug his heels into the flanks of the fat old horse, cantering off into the darkness where just a hint of dawn glowed on the edges of the hills far ahead.

The constable chewed on the end of his cigar. "Humph," he said to his horse. "Did you get a gander at that suit of clothes? Oh, well, it takes all kinds, as they say." And he followed slowly after, yawning, the gap between him and the man ahead lengthening with every mile.

Chapter 17

FOR THE SECOND MORNING in a row, Winnie Foster woke early. Outside, in the ring of trees around the pond, the birds were celebrating, giving the new day a brass band's worth of greeting. Winnie freed herself from the twisted quilt and went to a window. Mist lay on the surface of the water, and the light was still pale. It looked unreal, and she felt, herself, unreal, waking where she had, with her hair wild and her dress all crumpled. She rubbed her eyes. Through the dewy weeds below the window, a toad hopped suddenly into view and Winnie peered at it eagerly. But no—of course it wasn't the same toad. And remembering that other toad—*her* toad, she thought now, almost fondly—it seemed to her that she had been away from home for weeks. Then she heard a step on the loft stairs and thought, "Jesse!" At once her cheeks flamed.

But it was Miles. He came into the parlor, and when he saw that she was up, he smiled and whispered, "Good! you're awake. Come on—you can help me catch some fish for breakfast."

This time, Winnie was careful not to make a noise when she climbed into the rowboat. She made her way to her seat in the stern, and Miles handed her two old cane poles—"Watch out for the hooks!" he warned—and a jar of bait: pork fat cut into little pieces. A big brown night moth fluttered out from under the oar blades propped beside her on the seat, and wobbled off toward nowhere through the fragrant air. And from the bank, something plopped into the water. A frog! Winnie caught just a glimpse of it as it scissored away from shore. The water was so clear that she could see tiny brown fish near the bottom, flicking this way and that.

Miles pushed the rowboat off and sprang in, and soon they were gliding up toward the near end of the pond, where the water came in from the stream. The locks grated as the oars dipped and swung, but Miles was skillful. He rowed without a single splash. The dripping from the blades, as they lifted, sent rows of overlapping circles spreading silently behind them. It was very peaceful. "They'll take me home today," thought Winnie. She was somehow certain of this, and began to feel quite cheerful. She had been kidnapped, but nothing bad had happened, and now it was almost over. Now, remembering the visits of the night before, she smiled—and found that she loved them, this most peculiar family. They were her friends, after all. And hers alone.

"How'd you sleep?" Miles asked her.

"All right," she said.

"That's good. I'm glad. Ever been fishing before?"

"No," she told him.

"You'll like it. It's fun." And he smiled at her.

The mist was lifting now, as the sun poked up above the trees, and the water sparkled. Miles guided the rowboat near a spot where lily pads lay like upturned palms on the surface. "We'll let her drift some here," he said. "There'll be trout down in those weeds and stems. Here—give me the poles and I'll bait the hooks for us."

Winnie sat watching him as he worked. His face was like Jesse's, and yet not like. It was thinner, without Jesse's rounded cheeks, and paler, and his hair was almost straight, clipped neatly below the ears. His hands were different, too, the fingers thicker, the skin scrubbed-looking, but black at the knuckles and under the nails. Winnie remembered then that he worked sometimes as a blacksmith, and indeed his shoulders, under his threadbare shirt, were broad and muscled. He looked solid, like an oar, whereas Jesse—well, she decided, Jesse was like water: thin, and quick.

Miles seemed to sense that she was watching him. He looked up from the bait jar and his eyes, returning her gaze, were soft. "Remember I told you I had two children?" he asked. "Well, one of 'em was a girl. I took her fishing, too." His face clouded then, and he shook his head. "Her name was Anna. Lord, how sweet she was, that child! It's queer to think she'd be close to eighty now, if she's even still alive. And my son—he'd be eighty-two."

Winnie looked at his young, strong face, and after a moment she said, "Why didn't you take them to the spring and give them some of the special water?"

"Well, of course, we didn't realize about the spring while we was still on the farm." said Miles. "Afterwards, I thought about going to find them. I wanted to, heaven knows. But, Winnie, how'd it have been if I had? My wife was nearly forty by then. And the children—well, what was the use? They'd have been near growed theirselves.

They'd have had a pa close to the same age *they* was. No, it'd all have been so mixed up and peculiar, it just wouldn't have worked. Then Pa, he was dead-set against it, anyway. The fewer people know about the spring, he says, the fewer there are to tell about it. Here—here's your pole. Just ease the hook down in the water. You'll know when you get a bite."

Winnie clutched her pole, sitting sidewise in the stern, and watched the baited hook sink slowly down. A dragonfly, a brilliant blue jewel, darted up and paused over the lily pads, then swung up and away. From the nearest bank, a bullfrog spoke.

"There certainly are a lot of frogs around here," Winnie observed.

"That's so," said Miles. "They'll keep coming too, long as the turtles stay away. Snappers, now, they'll eat a frog soon as look at him."

Winnie thought about this peril to the frogs, and sighed. "It'd be nice," she said, "if nothing ever had to die."

"Well, now, I don't know," said Miles. "If you think on it, you come to see there'd be so many creatures, including people, we'd all be squeezed in right up next to each other before long."

Winnie squinted at her fishing line and tried to picture a teeming world. "Mmm," she said, "yes, I guess you're right."

Suddenly the cane pole jerked in her hands and bent into an arch, its tip dragged down nearly to the water's surface. Winnie held on tight to the handle, her eyes wide.

"Hey!" cried Miles. "Look, there! You got a bite. Fresh trout for breakfast, Winnie."

But just as suddenly the pole whipped straight again and the line went slack. "Shucks," said Miles. "it got away."

"I'm kind of glad," Winnie admitted, easing her grip on the butt of the pole. "*You* fish, Miles. I'm not so sure I want to."

And so they drifted for a little longer. The sky was blue and hard now, the last of the mist dissolved, and the sun, stepping higher above the trees, was hot on Winnie's back. The first week of August was re-asserting itself after a good night's sleep. It would be another searing day.

A mosquito appeared and sat down on Winnie's knee. She slapped at it absently, thinking about what Miles had said. If all the mosquitoes lived forever—and if they kept on having babies!—it would be terrible. The Tucks were right. It was best if no one knew about the spring, including the mosquitoes. She would keep the secret. She looked at Miles, and then she asked him, "What will you do, if you've got so much time?"

"Someday," said Miles, "I'll find a way to do something important."

Winnie nodded. That was what *she* wanted.

"The way I see it," Miles went on, "it's no good hiding yourself away, like Pa and lots of other people. And it's no good just thinking of your own pleasure, either. People got to do something useful if they're going to take up space in the world."

"But what will you *do?*" Winnie persisted.

"I don't know yet," said Miles. "I ain't had no schooling or nothing, and that makes it harder." Then he set his jaw and added, "I'll find a way, though, I'll locate something."

Winnie nodded. She reached out and ran her fingers across a lily pad that lay on the water beside the boat. It was warm and very dry, like a blotter, but near its center was a single drop of water, round and perfect. She touched the drop and brought her fingertip back wet: but the drop of water, though it rolled a little, remained as round and perfect as before.

And then Miles caught a fish. There it flopped, in the bottom of the boat, its jaw working, its gills fanning rapidly. Winnie drew up her knees and stared at it. It was beautiful, and horrible, too, with gleaming, rainbow-colored scales, and an eye like a marble beginning to dim even as she watched it. The hook was caught in its upper lip, and suddenly Winnie wanted to weep. "Put it back, Miles," she said, her voice dry and harsh. "Put it back right away."

Miles started to protest, and then, looking at her face, he picked up the trout and gently worked the barbed hook free. "All right, Winnie," he said. He dropped the fish over the edge of the boat. It flipped its tail and disappeared under the lily pads.

"Will it be all right?" asked Winnie, feeling foolish and happy both at once.

"It'll be all right," Miles assured her. And then he said, "People got to be meat-eaters, sometimes, though. It's the natural way. And that means killing things."

"I know," said Winnie weakly. "But still."

"Yes," said Miles. "I know."

Chapter 18

AND SO there were flapjacks again for breakfast, but no one seemed to mind. "Didn't get a bite?" said Mae.

"No," said Miles, "nothing we wanted to keep."

That was true, anyway. And though Winnie blushed as he said it, she was grateful that he didn't explain.

"Never mind," said Mae. "You're likely out of practice. Tomorrow, maybe."

"Sure," said Miles, "Tomorrow."

But it was the thought of seeing Jesse again that kept Winnie's stomach fluttering. And at last he came down from the loft, yawning and rosy, rubbing his curls, just as Mae was piling the plate with flapjacks. "Well, slug-a-bed," she said to him fondly. "You come near to missing breakfast. Miles and Winnie been up for hours, out fishing and back already."

"Oh?" said Jesse, his eyes on Miles. "Where's the fish, then? How come we got nothing but flapjacks?"

"No luck," said Mae. "They wasn't biting, for some reason."

"Reason is, Miles don't know how to fish," said Jesse. He grinned at Winnie and she lowered her eyes, her heart thumping.

"It don't matter," said Mae. "We got plenty without. Come and get your plates everybody."

They sat about in the parlor, as they had the night before. The ceiling swam with bright reflections, and sunlight streamed across the dusty, chip-strewn floor. Mae surveyed it all and sighed contentedly. "Now, this is real nice," she said, her fork poised above her place. "Everyone sitting down together. And having Winnie here—why it's just like a party."

"That's the truth," said Jesse and Miles both together, and Winnie felt a rush of happiness.

"Still, we got things to discuss," Tuck reminded them. "There's the business of the horse getting stole. And we got to get Winnie home where she belongs. How we going to do that without the horse?"

"After breakfast, Tuck," said Mae firmly. "Don't spoil a good meal with a lot of talk. We'll get to it soon enough."

So they were silent, eating, and this time Winnie licked the syrup from her fingers without pausing to think about it first. Her fears at last night's supper seemed silly to her now. Perhaps they *were* crazy, but they weren't criminals. She loved them. They belonged to her.

Tuck said, "How'd you sleep, child?"

And she answered, "Just fine," and wished, for a fleeting moment, that she could stay with them forever in that sunny, untidy little house by the pond. Grow up with them and perhaps, if it was true about the spring—then perhaps, when she was seventeen . . . She glanced at Jesse, where he sat on the floor, his curly head bent over his plate. Then she looked at Miles. And then her eyes went to Tuck and lingered on his sad, creased face. It occurred to her that he was the dearest of them all, though she couldn't have explained why she felt that way.

However, there wasn't time to wonder, for at that moment someone knocked at the door.

It was such an alien sound, so sudden and surprising, that Mae dropped her fork, and everyone looked up, startled. "Who's that?" said Tuck.

"I can't imagine," whispered Mae. "We ain't never had callers in all the years we been here."

The knock came again.

"I'll go Ma," said Miles.

"No. stay where you are," she said. "*I'll* go." She put her plate down carefully on the floor and stood up straightening her skirts. Then she went to the kitchen and opened the door.

Winnie recognized the voice at once. It was a rich and pleasant voice. The man in the yellow suit. And he was saying, "Good morning, Mrs. Tuck. It *is* Mrs. Tuck, isn't it? May I come in?"

Chapter 19

THE MAN IN THE YELLOW SUIT came into the sunlit parlor. He stood for a moment, looking around at them all, Mae and Miles and Jesse and Tuck, and Winnie, too. His face was without expression, but there was something unpleasant behind it that Winnie sensed at once, something that made her instantly suspicious. And yet his voice was mild when he said, "You're safe now, Winifred. I've come to take you home."

"We was going to bring her back directly, ourself," said Tuck, standing up slowly. "She ain't been in no danger."

"You're Mr. Tuck, I suppose," said the man in the yellow suit.

"I am," said Tuck, formally, his back straighter than usual.

"Well, you may as well sit down again. You, too, Mrs. Tuck. I have a great deal to say and very little time for saying it."

Mae sat down on the edge of the rocker, and Tuck sat, too, but his eyes were narrowed.

Jesse said, uneasily. "Who in tarnation do you think you—"

But Tuck interrupted. "Hush, boy. Let him speak his piece."

"That's wise," said the man in the yellow suit. "I'll be as brief as possible." He took off his hat and laid it on the mantel, and then he stood tapping his foot on the littered hearth, facing them. His face was smooth and empty. "I was born west of here," he began, "and all the time I was growing up, my grandmother told me stories. They were wild, unbelievable stories, but *I* believed them. They involved a dear friend of my grandmother's who married into a very odd family. Married the older of the two sons, and they had two children. It was after the children were born that she began to see that the family was odd. This friend of my grandmother's, she lived with her husband for twenty years, and strange to say, he never got any older. *She* did, but he didn't. And neither did his mother or his father or his brother. People began to wonder about that family, and my grandmother's friend decided at last that they were witches, or worse. She left her husband and came with her children to live at my grandmother's house for a short while. Then she moved west. I don't know what became of her. But my mother still remembers playing with the children. They were all about the same age. There was a son, and a daughter."

"Anna!" whispered Miles.

Mae burst out, "You got no call to come and bring us pain!"

And Tuck added roughly, "You got something to say, you better come to the point and say it."

"There, there, now," said the man in the yellow suit. He spread his long, white fingers in a soothing gesture. "Hear me out. As I've told you, I was fascinated by my grandmother's stories. People who never grew older! It was fantastic. It took possession of me. I decided to devote my life to finding out if it could be true, and if so, how and why. I went to school, I went to a university, I studied philosophy, metaphysics, and even a little medicine. None of it did me any good. Oh, there were ancient legends, but nothing more. I nearly gave it up. It began to seem ridiculous, and a waste of time. I went home. My grandmother was very old by then. I took her a present one day, a music box. And when I gave it to her, it reminded her of something: the woman, the mother of the family that didn't grow old, *she* had had a music box."

Mae's hand went to the pocket of her skirt. Her mouth opened, and then she shut it again with a snap.

"That music box played a very particular tune," the man in the yellow suit went on. "My grandmother's friend and her children—Anna? Was that the daughter's name?—they'd heard it so often that they knew it by heart. They'd taught it to my mother during the short time they lived in the house. We talked about it then, all those years afterward, my mother, my grandmother, and I. My mother was able to remember the melody, finally. She taught it to me. That was nearly twenty years ago now, but I kept it in my head. It was a clue."

The man in the yellow suit folded his arms and rocked a little. His voice was easy, almost friendly. "During those twenty years," he said, "I worked at other things. But I couldn't forget the tune or the family that didn't grow older. They haunted my dreams. So a few months ago I left my home and I started out to look for them, following the route they were said to have taken when they left their farm. No one I asked along the way knew anything. No one, had heard of them, no one recognized their name. But two evenings ago, I heard that music box, I heard that very tune, and it was coming from the Fosters' wood.

And the next morning early, I saw the family at last, taking Winifred away. I followed, and I heard their story, every word."

Mae's face drained of color. Her mouth hung open. And Tuck said hoarsely, "What are you going to do?"

The man in the yellow suit smiled. "The Fosters have given me the wood," he said. "In exchange for bringing Winifred home. I was the only one who knew where she was, you see. So it was a trade. Yes, I followed you, Mrs. Tuck, and then I took your horse and went directly back."

The tension in the parlor was immense. Winnie found that she could scarcely breathe. It *was* true, then! Or was the man who stood there crazy, too?

"Horse thief!" cried Tuck. "Get to the point! What are you going to do?"

"It's very simple," said the man in the yellow suit. And, as he said this, the smoothness of his face began to loosen a little. A faint flush crept up his neck, and the pitch of his voice lifted, became a fraction higher. "Like all magnificent things, it's very simple. The wood—and the spring—belong to me now." He patted his breast pocket. "I have a paper here, all signed and legal, to prove it. I'm going to sell the water, you see."

"You can't do that!" roared Tuck. "You got to be out of your mind!"

The man in the yellow suit frowned. "But I'm not going to sell it to just anybody," he protested. "Only to certain people, people who deserve it. And it will be very, very expensive. But who wouldn't give a fortune to live forever?"

"I wouldn't," said Tuck grimly.

"Exactly," said the man in the yellow suit. His eyes glowed. "Ignorant people like you should never have the opportunity. It should be kept for . . . certain others. And for me. However, since it's already too late to keep you out, you may as well join me in what I'm going to do. You can show me where the spring is and help me advertise. We'll set up demonstrations. You know—things that would be fatal to anybody else, but won't affect you in the least. I'll pay for your assistance, of course. It won't take long for the word to spread. And then you can go on your way. Well, what do you say?"

Jesse said dully, "Freaks. You want us to be freaks. In a patent medicine show."

The man in the yellow suit raised his eyebrows and a nervous petulance came into his voice. "Of course, if the idea doesn't appeal to you," he said, blinking rapidly, "you needn't be in on it. I can find the spring and manage just as well without you. But it seemed the gentlemanly thing to make the offer. After all," he added, looking round at the cluttered room, "it would mean you could afford to live like people again, instead of pigs."

And that was when the tension burst. All four Tucks sprang to their feet at once, while Winnie, very frightened, shrank back in her chair. Tuck cried, "You're a madman! A loony! You can't let *no* one know about the water. Don't you see what would *happen?*"

"I've given you your chance," shrilled the man in the yellow suit, "and you've refused it." He seized Winnie roughly by the arm and dragged her up out of her chair. "I'll take the child, and be on about my business."

Tuck began to rave now, his face stretched with horror. "Madman!" he shouted. And Miles and Jesse began to shout, too. They crowded after as the man in the yellow suit dragged Winnie through the kitchen to the door.

"No!" she was screaming, for now at last she hated him. "I won't go with you! I won't!"

But he opened the door and pushed her out in front of him. His eyes were like blind firepoints, his face twisted.

Then the shouting behind them stopped abruptly, and in the midst of the sudden silence came Mae's voice, flat and cold. "You leave that child be," she said.

Winnie stared. Mae was standing just outside the doorway. She held Tuck's long-forgotten shotgun by the barrel, like a club.

The man in the yellow suit smiled a ghastly smile. "I can't think why you're so upset. Did you really believe you could keep that water for yourselves? Your selfishness is really quite extraordinary, and worse than that, you're stupid. You could have done what I'm about to do, long ago. Now it's too late. Once Winifred drinks some of the water, she'll do just as well for my demonstrations. Even better. Children are much more appealing, anyway. So you may as well relax. There's nothing you can do to stop me."

But he was wrong. Mae lifted the shotgun. Behind her, Miles gasped, "Ma! *No!*"

But Mae's face was dark red. "Not Winnie!" she said between clenched teeth. "You ain't going to do a thing like that to Winnie.

And you ain't going to give out the secret." Her strong arms swung the shotgun round her head, like a wheel. The man in the yellow suit jerked away, but it was too late. With a dull cracking sound, the stock of the shotgun smashed into the back of his skull. He dropped like a tree, his face surprised, his eyes wide open. And at that very moment, riding through the pine trees just in time to see it all, came the Treegap constable.

Chapter 20

WINNIE WAS STANDING with her cheek pressed into Tuck's chest, her arms flung tight around him. She trembled, and kept her eyes squeezed shut. She could feel Tuck's breath come and go in little gasps. It was very quiet.

The Treegap constable knelt over the sprawled body of the man in the yellow suit, and then he said, "He ain't dead. Leastways, not yet."

Winnie opened her eyes a crack. She could see the shotgun lying on the grass where Mae had dropped it. She could see Mae's hands, too, hanging limp, clenching, then hanging limp again. The sun was scorching hot, and near her ear a gnat whined.

The constable stood up. "What did you hit him for?" he wheezed resentfully.

"He was taking the child away," said Mae. Her voice was dull and exhausted. "He was taking the child against her will."

At this the constable exploded. "Ding-dang it, woman, what you trying to say? Taking that child against her will? That's what *you* done. You *kidnapped* that child."

Winnie let go of Tuck's waist and turned around. Her trembling had stopped. "They didn't kidnap me," she said. "I came because I wanted to."

Behind her, Tuck drew his breath in sharply.

"You wanted to?" echoed the constable, his eyes wide with disbelief. "You *wanted* to?"

"That's right," said Winnie unflinchingly. "They're my friends."

The constable stared at her. He scratched his chin, eyebrows high, and eased his own shotgun to the ground. Then he shrugged and looked down at the man in the yellow suit, who lay motionless on the grass, the blazing sun white on his face and hands. His eyes were closed now, but except for that, he looked more than ever like a marionette, a marionette flung carelessly into a corner, arms and legs every which way midst tangled strings.

The one glance she gave him fixed his appearance forever in Winnie's mind. She turned her eyes away quickly, looking to Tuck for relief. But Tuck was not looking back at her. Instead, he was gazing at the body on the ground, leaning forward slightly, his brows drawn down, his mouth a little open. It was as if he were entranced and—yes, envious—like a starving man looking through a window at a banquet. Winnie could not bear to see him like that. She reached out a hand and touched him, and it broke the spell. He blinked and took her hand, squeezing it.

"Well, anyway," said the constable at last, turning businesslike. "I got to take charge here. Get this feller into the house before he fries. I'm telling you now: if he don't make it, you're in a pickle, you people. Now, here's what we'll do. You," he said, pointing at Mae, "you got to come with me, you and the little girl, I got to get her home. The rest of you, you stay here with him. Look after him. I'll get back with a doctor quick as I can. Should have brought a deputy, but I didn't expect nothing like this to happen. Well, it's too late now. All right, let's get moving."

Miles said softly, "Ma. We'll get you out right away."

"Sure, Ma," said Jesse.

"Don't worry about me none," said Mae in the same exhausted voice. "I'll make out."

"Make out?" exclaimed the constable. "You people beat all. If this feller dies, you'll get the gallows, that's what you'll get, if that's what you mean by make out."

Tuck's face crumpled. "The gallows?" he whispered. "Hanging?"

"That's it," said the constable. "That's the law. Now, let's get going."

Miles and Jesse lifted the man in the yellow suit and carried him carefully into the house, but Tuck stood staring, and Winnie could guess what he was thinking. The constable swung her up onto his horse and directed Mae to her own saddle. But Winnie kept her eyes on Tuck. His face was very pale, the creases deeper than ever, and his eyes looked blank and sunken. She heard him whisper again, "The gallows!"

And then Winnie said something she had never said before, but the words were words she had sometimes heard, and often longed to hear. They sounded strange on her own lips and made her sit up straighter. "Mr. Tuck," she said, "don't worry. Everything's going to be all right."

The constable glanced heavenward and shook his head. Then,

clutching his shotgun, he climbed up behind Winnie and turned the horse toward the path. "You first," he barked at Mae. "I got to keep an eye on you. And as for you," he added grimly, speaking to Tuck, "you better hope that feller don't die on you. I'll be back soon as I can."

"Everything'll be all right," Tuck repeated slowly.

Mae, slumped on the back of the fat old horse, did not respond. But Winnie leaned round the constable and looked back at Tuck. "You'll see," she said. And then she faced forward, sitting very straight. She was going home, but the thought of that was far from her mind. She watched the rump of the horse ahead, the swish of coarse, dusty hairs as he moved his tail. And she watched the swaying, sagging back of the woman who rode him.

Up through the dim pine trees they went, the constable's breath wheezing in her ears, and emerging from the coolness and the green, Winnie saw again the wide world spread before her, shimmering with light and possibility. But the possibilities were different now. They did not point to what might happen to her but to what she herself might keep from happening. For the only thing she could think of was the clear and terrible necessity: Mae Tuck must never go to the gallows. Whatever happened to the man in the yellow suit, Mae Tuck must not be hanged. Because if all they had said was true, then Mae, even if she were the cruelest of murderers and deserved to be put to death—Mae Tuck would not be able to die.

Chapter 21

WINNIE PULLED her little rocking chair up to her bedroom window and sat down. The rocking chair had been given to her when she was very small, but she still squeezed into it sometimes, when no one was looking, because the rocking made her almost remember something pleasant, something soothing, that would never quite come up to the surface of her mind. And tonight she wanted to be soothed.

The constable had brought her home. They had seized her at once, flinging the gate open and swooping down on her, her mother weeping, her father speechless, hugging her to him, her grandmother babbling with excitement. There was a painful pause when the constable told them she had gone away of her own free will, but it only lasted for a moment. They did not, would not believe it, and her grandmother said, "It was the elves. We heard them. They must have bewitched her."

And so they had borne her into the house, and after she had taken the bath they insisted upon, they fed and petted her and refused, with little laughs and murmurs, to accept her answers to their questions: She had gone away with the Tucks because—well, she wanted to. The Tucks had been very kind to her, had given her flapjacks, taken her fishing. The Tucks were good and gentle people. All this would have been swept away in any case, however, this good impression of her friends which she was trying to create, when she told them what had happened to the man in the yellow suit. Had they really given him the wood in exchange for finding her? They had. Well, perhaps he wouldn't want it now. Mae had hit him with the shotgun. He was very sick. They received this news with mingled hope and horror, and her father said, "I suppose the wood will be ours again if that man should . . . that is, if he doesn't . . ."

"You mean, if he dies," Winnie had said, flatly, and they had sat back, shocked. Soon after, they put her to bed, with many kisses. But they peered at her anxiously over their shoulders as they tiptoed out of her bedroom, as if they sensed that she was different now from what she had been before. As if some part of her had slipped away.

Well, thought Winnie, crossing her arms on the windowsill, she *was* different. Things had happened to her that were hers alone, and had nothing to do with them. It was the first time. And no amount of telling about it could help them understand or share what she felt. It was satisfying and lonely, both at once. She rocked, gazing out at the twilight, and the soothing feeling came reliably into her bones. That feeling—it tied her to them, to her mother, her father, her grand-mother, with strong threads too ancient and precious to be broken. But there were new threads now, tugging and insistent, which tie her just as firmly to the Tucks.

Winnie watched the sky slide into blackness over the wood out-side her window. There was not the least hint of a breeze to soften the heavy August night. And then, over the treetops, on the faraway horizon, there was a flash of white. Heat lightening. Again and again it throbbed, without a sound, It was like pain, she thought. And sud-denly she longed for a thunderstorm.

She cradled her head in her arms and closed her eyes. At once the image of the man in the yellow suit rose up. She could see him again, sprawled motionless on the sun-blanched grass. "He can't die," she whispered, thinking of Mae. "He mustn't." And then she considered his plans for the water in the spring, and Tuck's voice saying, "They'd all come running like pigs to slops." And she found herself thinking, "If it's true about the spring, then he has to die. He must. And that's why she did it."

Then she heard hoofbeats on the road below, a horse hurrying into the village, and not long after, there were footsteps and a knocking on the door. Winnie crept out of her room and crouched in the shadows at the top of the stairs. It was the constable. She heard him saying, "So that's that, Mr. Foster. We can't press no kidnapping charges, since your little girl claims there *wasn't* no kidnapping. But it don't matter now, anyway. The doc just got back a few minutes ago. That feller—the one you sold your land to? He's dead." There was a pause, and the murmur of other voices; then a match striking, the acrid smell of fresh cigar smoke. "Yep, she got him a good one, all right. He never even come to. So it's an open-and-shut case, since I seen her do it. Eyewitness. No question about it. They'll hang her for sure."

Winnie went back to her room and climbed into bed. She lay in the dark, propped up on the pillows, and stared at the lighter square of her window, at the heat lightning throbbing. It was like pain, she thought again, a dull pain on the fringes of the sky. Mae had killed the man in the yellow suit. And she had meant to kill him.

Winnie had killed a wasp once, in fear and anger, just in time to spare herself a stinging. She had slammed at the wasp with a heavy book, and killed it. And then, seeing its body broken, the thin wings stilled, she had wished it were alive again. She had wept for that wasp. Was Mae weeping now for the man in the yellow suit? In spite of her wish to spare the world, did she wish he were alive again? There was no way of knowing. But Mae had done what she thought she had to do. Winnie closed her eyes to shut out the silent pulsing of the lightning. Now *she* would have to do something. She had no idea what, but something. Mae Tuck must not go to the gallows.

Chapter 22

Next morning Winnie went out to the fence directly after breakfast. It was the hottest day yet, so heavy that the slightest exertion brought on a flood of perspiration, an exhaustion in the joints. Two days before, they would have insisted that she stay indoors, but now, this morning, they were careful with her, a little gingerly, as if she were an egg. She had said, "I'm going outside now," and they had said, "All right, but come in if it gets too hot, won't you, dear?" And she had answered, "Yes."

The earth, where it was worn bald under the gate, was cracked, and hard as rock, a lifeless tan color; and the road was an aisle of brilliant velvet dust. Winnie leaned against the fence, her hands gripping the warm metal of the bars, and thought about Mae behind another set of bars in the jailhouse. And then, lifting her head, she saw the toad. It was squatting where she had seen it first, across the road. "Hello!" she said, very glad to see it.

The toad did not so much as flick a muscle or blink an eye. It looked dried out today, parched. "It's thirsty," said Winnie to herself. "No wonder, on a day like this." She left the fence and went back into the cottage. "Granny, can I have some water in a dish? There's a toad out front that looks as if he's just about to die of thirst."

"A toad?" said her grandmother, wrinkling her nose in disgust. "Nasty things, toads."

"Not this one," said Winnie. "This one is always out there, and I like him. Can I give him a drink of water?"

"Toads don't drink water, Winifred. It wouldn't do him any good."

"They don't drink water at all?"

"No. They take it in through their skins, like a sponge. When it rains."

"But it hasn't rained forever!" said Winnie, alarmed. "I could sprinkle some water on him, couldn't I? That would help, wouldn't it?"

"Well, I suppose so," said her grandmother. "Where is he? In the yard?"

"No," said Winnie. "He's across the road."

"I'll come with you, then. I don't want you leaving the yard alone."

But when they came out to the fence, Winnie balancing a small bowl of water with enormous care, the toad was gone.

"Well, he must be all right," said her grandmother. "If he could hop off."

With mingled disappointment and relief, Winnie tipped the water onto the cracked earth at the gate. It was sucked in immediately, and the wet brown stain it left behind paled and vanished almost as quickly.

"I never saw such heat in all my life," said Winnie's grandmother, dabbing uselessly at her neck with a handkerchief. "Don't stay out here much longer."

"I won't," said Winnie, and was left alone once more. She sat down on the grass and sighed. Mae! What could she do to set Mae free? She closed her eyes against the glaring light, and watched, a little dizzily, as brilliant patterns of red and orange danced inside her eyelids.

And then, miraculously, Jesse was there, crouching just on the other side of the fence. "Winnie!" he hissed. "You sleeping?"

"Oh, Jesse!" Her eyes flew open and she reached through the fence to grasp his hand. "I'm so glad to see you! What can we do? We have to get her out!"

"Miles's got a plan, but I don't see how it can work," said Jesse, speaking quickly, his voice almost a whisper. "He knows a lot about carpentering. He says he can take Ma's window frame right straight out of the wall, bars and all, and she can climb through. We're going to try it tonight when it gets dark. Only trouble is, that constable keeps watching her every minute, he's so durned proud of having a prisoner in that new jail of his. We been down to see her. She's all right. But even if she can climb through the window, he'll come after her soon's he sees she's gone. Seems to me he'll notice right off. That don't give us much time to get away. But we got to try it. There ain't no other way. Anyhow, I come to say goodbye. We won't be able to come back here for a long, long time, Winnie, if we get away. I mean, they'll be looking for Ma. Winnie, listen—I won't see you again, not for ages. Look now—here's a bottle of water from the spring. You keep it. And then, no matter where you are, when you're seventeen,

Winnie , you can drink it, and then come find us. We'll leave directions somehow. Winnie, please say you will!"

He pressed the little bottle into her hands and Winnie took it, closing her fingers over it. "Jesse, wait!" she whispered breathlessly, for all at once she had the answer. "I can help! When your mother climbs out the window, I'll climb in and take her place. I can wrap myself up in her blanket, and when the constable looks in, he won't be able to tell the difference. Not in the dark. I can hump up and look a lot bigger. Miles can even put the window back. That would give you time to get away! You'd have at least till morning!"

Jesse squinted at her, and then he said, "Yep—you know, it might work. It might just make the difference. But I don't know as Pa's going to want you taking any risk. I mean, what'll they say to you after, when they find out?"

"I don't know," said Winnie, "but it doesn't matter. Tell your father, I want to help. I *have* to help. If it wasn't for me, there wouldn't have been any trouble in the first place. Tell him I have to."

"Well . . . all right. Can you get out after dark?"

"Yes," said Winnie.

"Then—at midnight, Winnie. I'll be waiting for you right here at midnight."

"Winifred!" an anxious voice called from the cottage. "Who's that you're talking to?"

Winnie stood up and turned to answer. "It's just a boy, Granny. I'll be in in a minute." When she turned around again, Jesse was gone. Winnie clutched the little bottle in her hands and tried to control the rising excitement that made her breath catch. At midnight she would make a difference in the world.

Chapter 23

IT WAS THE LONGEST DAY: mindlessly hot, unspeakably hot, too hot to move or even think. The countryside, the village of Treegap, the wood—all lay defeated. Nothing stirred. The sun was a ponderous circle without edges, a roar without a sound, a blazing glare so thorough and remorseless that even in the Fosters' parlor, with curtains drawn, it seemed an actual presence. You could not shut it out.

Winnie's mother and grandmother sat plaintive all afternoon in the parlor, fanning themselves and sipping lemonade, their hair unsettled and their knees loose. It was totally unlike them, this lapse from gentility, and it made them much more interesting. But Winnie didn't stay with them. Instead, she took her own brimming glass to her room and sat in her little rocker by the window. Once she had hidden Jesse's bottle in a bureau drawer, there was nothing to do but wait. In the hall outside her room, the grandfather's clock ticked deliberately, unimpressed with anyone's impatience, and Winnie found herself rocking to its rhythm—forward, back, forward, back, tick, tock, tick, tock, She tried to read, but it was so quiet that she could not concentrate, and so she was glad when at last it was time for supper. It was something to do, though none of them could manage more than a nibble.

But later, when Winnie went out again to the fence, she saw that the sky was changing. It was not so much clouding up as thickening, somehow from every direction at once, the blank blue gone to haze. And then, as the sun sank reluctantly behind the treetops, the haze hardened to a brilliant brownish-yellow. In the wood, the leaves turned underside-up, giving the trees a silvery cast.

The air was noticeably heavier. It pressed on Winnie's chest and made her breathing difficult. She turned and went back into the cottage. "It's going to rain, I think," she told the prostrate group in the parlor, and the news was received with little moans of gratitude.

Everyone went to bed early, closing windows firmly on their way. For outside, though it was almost dark, shreds of the hard brown-yellow light lingered on the rim of things, and there was a wind beginning, small gusts that rattled the fence gate and set the trees to rustling. The smell of rain hung sweet in the air. "What a week *this* has been!" said Winnie's grandmother. "Well, thank the Lord, it's almost over." And Winnie thought to herself: Yes, it's almost over.

There were three hours to wait before midnight and nothing whatever to do. Winnie wandered restlessly about her room, sat in her rocker, lay on her bed, counted the ticks of the hall clock. Beneath her excitement, she was thick with guilt. For the second time in three short days—though they seemed many more than that—she was about to do something which she knew would be forbidden. She didn't have to ask.

Winnie had her own strong sense of rightness. She knew that she could always say, afterward, "Well, you never told me *not* to!" But how silly that would be! Of course it would never occur to them to include such a thing on their list of don'ts. She could hear them saying it, and almost smiled: "Now, remember, Winifred—don't bite your fingernails, don't interrupt when someone else is speaking, and don't go down to the jailhouse at midnight to change places with prisoners."

Still, it wasn't really funny. What would happen in the morning, when the constable found her in the cell and had to bring her home for the second time? What would they say? Would they ever trust her again? Winnie squirmed, sitting in the rocker, and swallowed uncomfortably. Well, she would have to make them understand, somehow, without explaining.

The hall clock chimed eleven. Outside, the wind had stopped. Everything, it seemed, was waiting. Winnie lay down and closed her eyes. Thinking of Tuck and Mae, of Miles and Jesse, her heart softened. They needed her. To take care of them. For in the funny sort of way that had struck her at the first, they were helpless. Or too trusting. Well, *something* like that. Anyway, they needed her. She would not disappoint them. Mae would go free. No one would have to find out—Winnie would not have to find out—that Mae could not . . . but Winnie blocked the picture from her mind, the horror that would prove the secret. Instead, she turned her thoughts to Jesse. When she was seventeen—would she? If it was true, would she? And if she did, would she be sorry afterwards? Tuck had said, "It's something you don't find out how you feel until afterwards." But no—it wasn't true. She knew that, now, here in her own bedroom. They were probably crazy after all. But she loved them anyway. They needed her. And, thinking this Winnie fell asleep.

She woke with a jerk sometime later, and sat up, alarmed. The clock was ticking steadily, the darkness was complete. Outside, the night seemed poised on tiptoe, waiting, waiting, holding its breath for the storm. Winnie stole out to the hall and frowned at the clock face in the shadows. And at last she could make it out, for the black Roman numerals were just barely visible against their white ground, the brass hands glowed faintly. As she peered at them, the long hand snapped forward one more notch, with a loud click. She had not missed her moment—it was five minutes to midnight.

Chapter 24

LEAVING THE HOUSE was so easy that Winnie felt faintly shocked. She had half expected that the instant she put a foot on the stairs they would leap from their beds and surround her with accusations. But no one stirred. And she was struck by the realization that, if she chose, she could slip out night after night without their knowing. The thought made her feel more guilty than ever that she could once more take advantage of their trust. But tonight, this one last time, she had to. There was no other way. She opened the door and slipped out into the heavy August night.

Leaving the cottage was like leaving something real and moving into dream. Her body felt weightless, and she seemed to float down the path to the gate. Jesse was there, waiting. Neither of them spoke. He took her and they ran together, lightly, down the road, past other sleeping cottages, into the dim and empty center of the village. The big glass windows here were lidded eyes that didn't care—that barely saw them, barely gave them back reflections. The blacksmith's shop, the mill, the church, the stores, so busy and alive in the daylight, were hunched, deserted now, dark piles and shapes without a purpose or a meaning. And then, ahead, Winnie saw the jailhouse, its new wood still unpainted, lamplight spilling through a window at the front. And there, in the cleared yard behind it, like a great L upside down, was the gallows.

The sky flashed white. But this time it wasn't heat lightning, for a few moments later a low mumble, still far away, announced at last the coming storm. A fresh breeze lifted Winnie's hair, and from somewhere in the village behind them a dog barked.

Two shadows detached themselves from the gloom as Winnie and Jesse came up. Tuck pulled her to him and hugged her hard, and Miles squeezed her hand. No one said a word. Then the four of them crept to the back of the building. Here, too high for Winnie to see into, was a barred window through which, from the room in front, light glowed faintly. Winnie peered up at it, at the blackness of the bars with the dim gold of the light between. Into her head came lines from an old poem:

> Stone walls do not a prison make,
> Nor iron bars a cage.

Over and over the lines repeated themselves in her head till they were altogether meaningless. Another roll of thunder sounded. The storm was moving nearer.

Then Miles was standing on a box. He was pouring oil around the frame of the window. A swirl of wind brought the thick, rich smell of it down to Winnie's nostrils. Tuck handed up a tool and Miles began to pry at the nails securing the window frame. Miles knew carpentering. Miles could do the job. Winnie shivered and held tight to Jesse's hand. One nail was free. Another. Tuck reached up to receive them as they came out one by one. A fourth nail screeched as it was pried up, and Miles poured on more oil.

From the front of the jailhouse, the constable yawned noisily and began to whistle. The whistling came nearer. Miles dropped down. They heard the constable's footsteps coming to Mae's cell. The barred door clanked. Then the footsteps receded, the whistling grew fainter. An inner door shut, and the lamp glow disappeared.

At once Miles was up again and prying at the nails. An eighth was out, a ninth, a tenth. Winnie counted carefully, while behind her counting, her mind sang, "Stone walls do not a prison make."

Miles handed down the prying tool. He grasped the bars of the window firmly, ready to pull, and stood poised. "What is he waiting for?" thought Winnie. "Why doesn't he . . ." Then—a flash of lightning, and soon after, a crack of thunder. In the midst of the noise, Miles gave a mighty heave. But the window did not budge.

The thunder ebbed. Winnie's heart sank. What if it was all impossible? What if the window would never come out? What if . . . She looked over her shoulder at the dark shape of the gallows, and shuddered.

Again a flash of lightning, and this time a crashing burst of noise from the swirling sky. Miles yanked. The window frame sprang free, and still grasping it by the bars, he tumbled backward off the box. The job was done.

Two arms appeared in the hole left by the missing frame. Mae! Her head appeared. It was too dark to see her face. The window—what if it was too small for her to squeeze through? What if . . . But now her shoulders were out. She groaned softly. Another flash of lightning lit her face for an instant and Winnie saw an expression there of deep concentration, tip of tongue protruding, brows furrowed.

Now Tuck was on the box, helping her, giving her his own shoulders to pull on, Miles and Jesse close at his sides, arms upstretched, eager to receive her bulk. Her hips were free—now, look out!—here she came, her skirts tearing on the rough edges of the boards, arms flailing—and they were all in a heap on the ground. Another crash of thunder muffled Jesse's bursting, exultant laugh. Mae was free.

Winnie clasped her trembling hands thankfully. And then the first drop of rain plopped precisely on the tip of her nose. The Tucks untangled themselves and turned to her. One by one, as the rain began, they drew her to them and kissed her. One by one she kissed them back. Was it rain on Mae's face? On Tuck's? Or was it tears? Jesse was last. He put his arms around her and hugged her tight, and whispered the single word, "Remember!"

Then Miles was on the box again, lifting her. Her hands grasped the edges of the window. This time she waited with him. When the thunder came, it tore the sky apart with its roar, as it came, she pulled herself through, and dropped on the cot inside, unharmed. She looked up at the open square and saw the frame with Mile's hands holding it. The next obliging roll of thunder saw it wedged once more into place. And then—would Miles put back the nails? She waited.

Rain came in sheets now, riding the wind, flung crosswise through the night. Lightning crackled, a brilliant, jagged streak, and thunder rattled the little building. The tension in the parched earth eased and vanished. Winnie felt it go. The muscles of her stomach loosened, and all at once she was exhausted.

Still she waited. Would Miles put back the nails? At last, standing on tiptoe on the cot, she grasped the bars of the window, pulling herself up till she could see through. Rain blew into her face, but at the next flash of lightning, looking down, she saw the yard was empty. And before the thunder followed, in a pause while wind and rain held back for one brief moment, she thought she heard, fading in the distance, the tinkling little melody of the music box. The Tucks—her darling Tucks—were gone.

Chapter 25

THE FIRST WEEK of August was long over. And now, though autumn was still some weeks away, there was a feeling that the year had begun its downward arc, that the wheel was turning again, slowly now, but soon to go faster, turning once more in its changeless sweep of change. Winnie, standing at the fence in the front of the touch-me-not cottage, could hear the new note in the voices of the birds. Whole clouds of them lifted, chattering, into the sky above the wood, and then settled, only to lift again. Across the road, goldenrod was coming into bloom. And an early-drying milkweed had opened its rough pod, exposing a host of downy-headed seeds. As she watched, one of these detached itself into a sudden breeze and sailed sedately off, while others leaned from the pod as if to observe its departure.

Winnie dropped down cross-legged on the grass. Two weeks had gone by since the night of the storm, the night of Mae Tuck's escape. And Mae had not been found. There was no trace of her at all, or Tuck or Miles or Jesse. Winnie was profoundly grateful for that. But she was also profoundly tired. It had been a trying two weeks.

For the hundredth time she reviewed it all: how the constable had come into the cell soon after she had settled herself on the cot; how he had let down a shutter over the window to keep out the rain; how, then, he had stood over her as she hunched under the blanket, her breath heavy, trying to look as large as possible; how, finally, he had gone away and not come back till morning.

But she had not dared to sleep, for fear she would kick off the blanket and give herself away—give the Tucks away—unwittingly. So she had lain there, pulse thudding, eyes wide open. She would never forget the rattle of the rain on the jailhouse roof, or the smell of wet wood, or the darkness that had saved them all; or how difficult it was not to cough. She had wanted to cough as soon as it occurred to her that she mustn't, and she passed a long hour trying to swallow away at the tickle that perversely constricted her throat. And she would never forget the crash outside that made her heart race, that she could not investigate, and did not understand till morning, when on the way home she saw that the gallows had blown over in the wind.

But oh!—it made her tremble still to remember the constable's face when he found her. She had heard first a bustling in the front of the jail, and smelled fresh coffee, and had sat up, stiff with apprehension. Then the inner door opened—the door, she now saw, which separated the office from the pair of cells—and in the light that streamed before him, the constable appeared, carrying a breakfast tray. He was whistling cheerfully. He came up to the barred door of her cell and looked in. And his whistling died on his lips as if it had run down and needed to be wound up again. But this comical astonishment lasted for a moment only. And then his face flushed red with anger.

Winnie had sat on the cot, eyes downcast, feeling very small— very criminal. In fact, he was soon shouting that if she were older, he'd have to keep her there—that it *was* a crime, what she had done. She was . . . an accomplice. She had helped a murderer escape. She was, in fact, a criminal. But too young to be punished by the law. Worse luck, he told her, for she badly needed punishing.

She was released, then, into the custody of her mother and father. And these new words, "accomplice" and "custody," chilled her blood. Over and over they asked her, shocked at first and then wistful: why had she *done* such a thing? *Why?* She was their daughter. They had trusted her. They had tried to bring her up properly, with a true sense of right and wrong. They did not understand. And finally she had sobbed the only truth there was into her mother's shoulder, the only explanation: the Tucks were her friends. She had done it because—in spite of everything, she loved them.

This of all things her family understood, and afterward they drew together staunchly around her. It was hard for them in the village. Winnie knew it was, and that knowledge gave her pain. For they were proud. And she had shamed them. Still, this side of the affair was not without its benefits, at least for Winnie. Though she was confined to the yard indefinitely and could go nowhere, not even with her mother or her grandmother, the other children wandered by to look at her, to talk to her through the fence. They were impressed by what she had done. She was a figure of romance to them now, where before she had been too neat, too prissy; almost, somehow, too *clean* to be a real friend.

Winnie sighed and plucked at the grass around her ankles. School would open soon. It wouldn't be so bad. In fact, she thought as her spirits lifted, this year it might be rather nice.

And then two things happened. First of all, the toad appeared out of the weeds, on her side of the road this time. It bounced out of a cover of old dandelion leaves and landed—plop!—just behind the fence. If she had reached her hand through the bars, she could have touched it. And next, a large brown dog, with easy gait and dangling tongue, came lopping down the road toward them. He stopped opposite the fence and looked at Winnie with a friendly swish of his tail, and then he saw the toad. At once he began to bark, his eyes bright. He pranced up, his hind quarters leaping independently from side to side, nose close to the toad, his voice shrill with enthusiasm.

"Don't!" cried Winnie, leaping to her feet and flapping her arms. "Go away, dog!" Stop that! Go away—shoo!"

The dog paused. He looked up at Winnie's frantic dancing and then he looked at the toad, who had pressed down close to the dirt, eyes tight shut. It was too much for him. He began to bark again, and reached out a long paw.

"Oh!" cried Winnie. "Oh—*don't* do that! Leave my toad *alone!*" And before she had time to realize what she was doing, she bent, reached through the bars, and snatched the toad up and away from harm, dropping it on the grass inside the fence.

A feeling of revulsion swept through her. While the dog whined, pawing uselessly at the fence, she stood rigid, staring at the toad, wiping her hand again and again on the skirt of her dress. Then she remembered the actual feel of the toad, and the revulsion passed. She knelt and touched the skin of its back. It was rough and soft, both at once. And cool.

Winnie stood up and looked at the dog. He was waiting outside the fence, his head on one side, peering at her longingly. "It's *my* toad," Winnie told him. "So you'd better leave it alone." And then, on an impulse, she turned and ran into the cottage, up to her room, to the bureau drawer where she had hidden Jesse's bottle—the bottle of water from the spring. In a moment she was back again. The toad still squatted where she had dropped it, the dog still waited at the fence. Winnie pulled out the cork from the mouth of the bottle, and kneeling, she poured the precious water, very slowly and carefully, over the toad.

The dog watched this operation, and then, yawning, he was suddenly bored. He turned and loped away, back down the road to the village. Winnie picked up the toad and held it for a long time, without the least disgust, in the palm of her hand. It sat calmly, blinking, and the water glistened on its back.

The little bottle was empty now. It lay on the grass at Winnie's feet. But if all of it was true, there was more water in the wood. There was plenty more. Just in case. When she was seventeen. If she should decide, there was more water in the wood. Winnie smiled. Then she stopped and put her hand through the fence and set the toad free. "There!" she said. "You're safe. Forever."

Epilogue

THE SIGN SAID *WELCOME TO TREEGAP*, but it was hard to believe that this was really Treegap. The main street hadn't changed so very much, but there were many other streets now, crossing the main street. The road itself was blacktopped. There was a white line painted down its center.

Mae and Tuck, on the seat of a clattering wooden wagon, bumped slowly into Treegap behind the fat old horse. They had seen continuous change and were accustomed to it, but here it seemed shocking and sad. "Look," said Tuck. "Look, Mae. Ain't that where the wood used to be? It's gone! Not a stick or a stump left! And her cottage—that's gone, to."

It was very hard to recognize anything, but from the little hill, which had once lain outside the village and was now very much a part of it, they thought they could figure things out. "Yes," said Mae, "that's where it was, I do believe. 'Course, it's been so long since we was here, I can't tell for certain."

There was a gas station there now. A young man in greasy overalls was polishing the windshield of a wide and rusty Hudson automobile. As Mae and Tuck rolled past, the young man grinned and said to the driver of the Hudson, who lounged at the wheel, "Looky here. In from the country for a big time." And they chuckled together.

Mae and Tuck clattered on into the village proper, past a catholic mixture of houses which soon gave way to shops and other places of business: a hot-dog stand; a dry cleaner; a pharmacy; a five-and-ten; another gas station; a tall, white frame building with a pleasant verandah, The Treegap Hotel—Family Dining, Easy Rates. The post office. Beyond that, the jailhouse, but a large jailhouse now, painted brown, with an office for the county clerk. A black and white police car was parked in front, with a red glass searchlight on its roof and a radio antenna, like a buggy whip, fastened to the windshield.

Mae glanced at the jailhouse, but looked away quickly. "See beyond there?" she said, pointing. "That diner? Let's stop there and get a cup of coffee. All right?"

"All right," said Tuck. "Maybe they'll know something."

Inside, the diner gleamed with chrome and smelled like linoleum and ketchup. Mae and Tuck took seats on rumbling swivel stools at the long counter. The counterman emerged from the kitchen at the rear and sized them up expertly. They looked all right. A little queer, maybe—their clothes, especially—but honest. He slapped a cardboard menu down in front of them and leaned on the foaming orangeade cooler. "You folks from off?" he asked.

"Yep," said Tuck. "Just passing through."

"Sure," said the counterman.

"Say," said Tuck cautiously, fingering the menu. "Didn't there used to be a wood once, down the other side of town?"

"Sure," said the counterman. "Had a big electrical storm, though, about three years ago now or thereabouts. Big tree got hit by lightning, split right down the middle. Caught fire and everything. Tore up the ground, too. Had to bulldoze her all out."

"Oh," said Tuck. He and Mae exchanged glances.

"Coffee, please," said Mae. "Black. For both of us."

"Sure," said the counterman. He took the menu away, poured coffee into thick pottery mugs, and leaned again on the orangeade cooler.

"Used to be a fresh-water spring in that wood," said Tuck boldly, sipping his coffee.

"Don't know nothing about that," said the counterman. "Had to bulldoze her all out, like I say."

"Oh," said Tuck.

Afterward, while Mae was shopping for supplies, Tuck went back through the town on foot—back the way they had come—out to the little hill. There were houses there now, and a feed-and-grain store, but on the far side of the hill, inside a rambling iron fence was a cemetery.

Tuck's heart quickened. He had noticed the cemetery on the way in. Mae had seen it, too. They had not spoken about it. But both knew it might hold other answers. Tuck straightened his old jacket. He passed through an archway of wrought-iron curlicues, and paused, squinting at the weedy rows of gravestones. And then, far over to the right, he saw a tall monument, once no doubt imposing but now tipped slightly sidewise. On it was carved one name: Foster.

Slowly, Tuck turned his footsteps toward the monument. And saw, as he approached, that there were other, smaller markers all around it. A family plot. And then his throat closed. For it was there. He had wanted it to be there, but now that he saw it, he was overcome with sadness. He knelt and read the inscription:

In Loving Memory
Winifred Foster Jackson
Dear Wife
Dear Mother
1870–1948

"So," said Tuck to himself. "Two years. She's been gone two years." He stood up and looked around embarrassed, trying to clear the lump from his throat. But there was no one to see him. The cemetery was very quiet. In the branches of a willow behind him, a red-winged blackbird chirped. Tuck wiped his eyes hastily. Then he straightened his jacket again and drew up his hand in a brief salute. "Good girl," he said aloud. And then he turned and left the cemetery, walking quickly.

Later, as he and Mae rolled out of Treegap, Mae said softly, without looking at him, "She's gone?"

Tuck nodded. "She's gone," he answered.

There was a long moment of silence between them, and then Mae said, "Poor Jesse."

"He knowed it, though," said Tuck. "At least, he knowed she wasn't coming. We all knowed that, long time ago."

"Just the same," said Mae. She sighed. And then she sat up a little straighter. "Well, where to now, Tuck? No need to come back here no more."

"That's so," said Tuck. "Let's just head on out this way. We'll locate something."

"All right," said Mae. And then she put a hand on his arm and pointed. "Look out for that toad."

Tuck had seen it, too. He reined in the horse and climbed down from the wagon. The toad was squatting in the middle of the road, quite unconcerned. In the other lane, a pickup truck rattled by, and against the breeze it made, the toad shut its eyes tightly. But it did not move. Tuck waited till the truck had passed, and then he picked up the toad and carried it to the weeds along the road's edge. "Durn fool thing must think it's going to live forever," he said to Mae.

And soon they were rolling on again, leaving Treegap behind, and as they went, the tinkling little melody of a music box drifted out behind them and was lost at last far down the road.

Related Readings

Ecclesiastes 3:1–8

This scripture from the Bible shares a lesson about life.

To EVERY THING THERE IS A SEASON, and a time to every purpose under the heaven:

2   A time to be born, and a time to die; a time to plant, and a time to pluck up that which is planted;

3   A time to kill, and a time to heal; a time to break down, and a time to build up;

4   A time to weep, and a time to laugh; a time to mourn, and a time to dance;

5   A time to cast away stones, and a time to gather stones together; a time to embrace, and a time to refrain from embracing;

6   A time to get, and a time to lose; a time to keep, and a time to cast away;

7   A time to rend, and a time to sew; a time to keep silence, and a time to speak;

8   A time to love, and a time to hate; a time of war, and a time of peace.

Merrill Moore

Fable

*These two readings deal with the theme of death and
the difficulty people have in dealing with the
knowledge of their own mortality.*

Does everyone have to die? *Yes, everyone.*
Isn't there some way I can arrange
Not to die—cannot I take some strange
Prescription that my physician might know of?

5 *No. I think not, not for money or love:*
Everyone has to die, yes, everyone.

Cannot my banker and his bank provide,
Like a trust fund, for me to live on inside
My warm bright house and not be put into
10 A casket in the clay, can they not do
That for me and charge a fixed per cent
Like interest or taxes or the rent?

No, Madame, I fear not, and if they could
There might be more harm in it than good.

The Weaver of Tomorrow

Jane Yolen

ONCE, on the far side of yesterday, there lived a girl who wanted to know the future. She was not satisfied with knowing that the grass would come up each spring and that the sun would go down each night. The true knowledge she desired was each tick of tomorrow, each fall and each failure, each heartache and each pain, that would be the portion of every man. And because of this wish of hers, she was know as Vera, which is to say *True*.

At first it was easy enough. She lived simply in a simple town, where little happened to change a day but a birth or a death that was always expected. And Vera awaited each event at the appointed bed-side and, in this way, was always the first to know.

But as with many wishes of the heart, hers grew from a wish to a desire, from a desire to an obsession. And soon, knowing the simple futures of the simple people in that simple town was not enough for her.

"I wish to know what tomorrow holds for everyone," said Vera. "For every man and woman in our country. For every man and woman in our world."

"It is not good, this thing you wish," said her father.

But Vera did not listen. Instead she said, "I wish to know which king will fall and what the battle, which queen will die and what the cause. I want to know how many mothers will cry for babies lost and how many wives will weep for husbands slain."

And when she heard this, Vera's mother made the sign against the Evil One, for it was said in their simple town that the future was the Devil's dream.

But Vera only laughed and said loudly, "And for that, I want to know what the Evil One himself is doing with *his* tomorrow."

Since the Evil One himself could not have missed her speech, the people of the town visited the Mayor and asked him to send Vera away.

The Mayor took Vera and her mother and father, and they sought out the old man who lived in the mountain who would answer one question a year. And they asked him what to do about Vera.

The old man who lived in the mountain, who ate the seeds that flowers dropped and the berries that God wrought, and who knew all about yesterdays and cared little about tomorrow, said, "She must be apprenticed to the Weaver." [1]

"A weaver!" said the Mayor and Vera's father and her mother all at once. They thought surely that the old man who lived in the mountain had at last gone mad.

But the old man shook his head. "Not a weaver, but *the* Weaver, the Weaver of Tomorrow. She weaves with a golden thread and finishes each piece with a needle so fine that each minute of the unfolding day is woven into her work. They say that once every hundred years there is need for an apprentice, and it is just that many years since one has been found."

"Where does one find this Weaver?" asked the Mayor.

"Ah, that I cannot say," said the old man who lived in the mountain, "for I have answered one question already." And he went back to his cave and rolled a stone across the entrance, a stone small enough to let the animals in but large enough to keep the townspeople out.

"Never mind," said Vera. "I would be apprenticed to this Weaver. And not even the Devil himself can keep me from finding her."

And so saying, she left the simple town with nothing but the clothes upon her back. She wandered until the hills got no higher but the valleys got deeper. She searched from one cold moon until the next. And at last, without warning, she came upon a cave where an old woman in black stood waiting.

"You took the Devil's own time coming," said the old woman.

"It was not his time at all," declared Vera.

"Oh, but it was," said the old woman, as she led the girl into the cave.

And what a wondrous place the cave was. On one wall hung skeins[2] of yarn of rainbow colors. On the other walls were tapestries of delicate design. In the center of the cave where a single shaft of

---

1. **be apprenticed to the Weaver** learn the Weaver's trade
2. **skeins** continuous strands of yarn or thread

sunlight fell was the loom of polished ebony,[3] higher than a man and three times as broad, with a shuttle that flew like a captive black bird through the golden threads of the warp.[4]

For a year and a day, Vera stayed in the cave apprenticed to the Weaver. She learned which threads wove the future of kings and princes and which of peasants and slaves. She was first to know in which kingdoms the sun would set and which kingdoms would be gone before the sun rose again. And though she was not yet allowed to weave, she watched the black loom where each minute of the day took shape, and learned how, once it had been woven, no power could change its course. Not an emperor, not a slave, not the Weaver herself. And she was taught to finish the work with a golden thread and a needle so fine that no one could tell where one day ended and the next began. And for a year she was happy.

But finally the day dawned when Vera was to start her second year with the Weaver. It began as usual. Vera rose and set the fire. Then she removed the tapestry of yesterday from the loom and brushed it outside until the golden threads mirrored the morning sun. She hung it on a silver hook that was by the entrance to the cave. Finally she returned to the loom which waited mutely for the golden warp to be strung. And each thread that Vera pulled tight sang like the string of a harp. When she was through, Vera set the pot on the fire and woke the old woman to begin weaving.

The old woman creaked and muttered as she stretched herself up. But Vera paid her no heed. Instead, she went to the Wall of Skeins and picked at random the colors to be woven. And each thread was a life.

"Slowly, slowly," the old Weaver had cautioned when Vera first learned to choose the threads. "At the end of each thread is the end of a heartbeat; the last of each color is the last of a world." But Vera could not learn to choose slowly, carefully. Instead she plucked and picked like a gay bird in the seed.

"And so it was with me," said the old Weaver with a sigh. "And so it was at first with me."

---

3. **ebony** a deep black wood
4. **warp** lengthwise threads in a woven fabric

Now a year had passed, and the old woman kept her counsel to herself as Vera's fingers danced through the threads. Now she went creaking and muttering to the loom and began to weave. And now Vera turned her back to the growing cloth that told the future and took the pot from the fire to make their meal. But as soon as that was done, she would hurry back to watch the growing work, for she never wearied of watching the minutes take shape on the ebony loom.

Only this day, as her back was turned, the old woman uttered a cry. It was like a sudden sharp pain. And the silence after it was like the release from pain altogether.

Vera was so startled she dropped the pot, and it spilled over and sizzled the fire out. She ran to the old woman who sat staring at the growing work. There, in the gold and shimmering tapestry, the Weaver had woven her own coming death.

There was the cave and there the dropped pot; and last the bed where, with the sun shining full on her face, the old woman would breathe no more.

"It has come," the old woman said to Vera, smoothing her black skirts over her knees. "The loom is yours." She stood up fresher and younger than Vera had ever seen her, and moved with a springy joy to the bed. Then she straightened the covers and lay down, her face turned toward the entrance of the cave. A shaft of light fell on her feet and began to move, as the sun moved, slowly towards her head.

"No," cried Vera at the smiling woman. "I want the loom. But not this way."

Gently, with folded hands, the old Weaver said, "Dear child, there is no other way."

"Then," said Vera slowly, knowing she lied, but lying nonetheless, "I do not want it."

"The time for choosing is past," said the old Weaver. "You chose and your hands have been chosen. It is woven. It is so."

"And in a hundred years?" asked Vera.

"You will be the Weaver, and some young girl will come, bright and eager, and you will know your time is near."

"No," said Vera.

"It is birth," said the old Weaver.

"No," said Vera.

"It is death," said the old Weaver.

A single golden thread snapped suddenly on the loom.

Then the sun moved onto the Weaver's face and she died.

Vera sat staring at the old woman but did not stir. And though she sat for hour upon hour, and the day grew cold, the sun did not go down. Battles raged on and on, but no one won and no one lost for nothing more had been woven.

At last, shivering with the cold, though the sun was still high, Vera went to the loom. She saw the old woman buried and herself at work, and so she hastened to the tasks.

And when the old woman lay under an unmarked stone in a forest full of unmarked stones, with only Vera to weep her down, Vera returned to the cave.

Inside, the loom gleamed black, like a giant ebony cage with golden bars as thin and fine as thread. And as Vera sat down to finish the weaving, her bones felt old and she welcomed the shaft of sun as it crept across her back. She welcomed each trip of the shuttle through the warp as it ticked off the hundred years to come. And at last Vera knew all she wanted to know about the future.

The Water
of Life

What are the results of selfishness and greed? This fairy tale—one of the well-known Grimm's Fairy Tales—shows what happens when someone thinks only about his or her best interests.

THERE WAS ONCE a King who had an illness, and no one believed that he would come out of it with his life. He had three sons who were much distressed about it, and went down into the palace-garden and wept. There they met an old man who inquired as to the cause of their grief. They told him that their father was so ill that he would most certainly die, for nothing seemed to cure him. Then the old man said: "I know of one more remedy, and that is the water of life; if he drinks of it he will become well again; but it is hard to find." The eldest said: "I will manage to find it," and went to the sick King, and begged to be allowed to go forth in search of the water of life, for that alone could save him. "No," said the King, "the danger of it is too great. I would rather die." But he begged so long that the King consented. The prince thought in his heart: "If I bring the water, then I shall be best beloved of my father, and shall inherit the kingdom." So he set out, and when he had ridden forth a little distance, a dwarf stood there in the road who called to him and said: "Whither away so fast?" "Silly shrimp," said the prince, very haughtily,[1] "it is nothing to do with you," and rode on. But the little dwarf had grown angry, and had wished an evil wish. Soon after this the prince entered a ravine,[2] and the further he rode the closer the mountains drew together, and at last the road became so narrow that he could not advance a step further; it was impossible either to turn

---

1. **haughtily** proudly; self-importantly
2. **ravine** canyon

his horse or to dismount from the saddle, and he was shut in there as if in prison. The sick King waited long for him, but he came not. Then the second son said: "Father, let me go forth to seek the water," and thought to himself: "If my brother is dead, then the kingdom will fall to me." At first the King would not allow him to go either, but at last he yielded, so the prince set out on the same road that his brother had taken, and he too met the dwarf, who stopped him to ask, whither he was going in such haste. "Little shrimp," said the prince, "that is nothing to do with you," and rode on without giving him another look. But the dwarf bewitched him, and he, like the other, rode into a ravine, and could neither go forwards nor backwards. So fare haughty people.

As the second son also remained away, the youngest begged to be allowed to go forth to fetch the water, and at last the King was obliged to let him go. When he met the dwarf and the latter asked him whither he was going in such haste, he stopped, gave him an explanation, and said: "I am seeking the water of life, for my father is sick unto death." "Do you know, then, where that is to be found?" "No," said the prince. "As you have borne yourself as is seemly, and not haughtily like your false brothers, I will give you the information and tell you how you may obtain the water of life. It springs from a fountain in the courtyard of an enchanted castle, but you will not be able to make your way to it, if I do not give you an iron wand and two small loaves of bread. Strike thrice with the wand on the iron door of the castle, and it will spring open: inside lie two lions with gaping jaws, but if you throw a loaf to each of them, they will be quieted. Then hasten to fetch some of the water of life before the clock strikes twelve, else the door will shut again, and you will be imprisoned." The prince thanked him, took the wand and the bread, and set out on his way. When he arrived, everything was as the dwarf had said. The door sprang open at the third stroke of the wand, and when he had appeased the lions with the bread, he entered the castle, and came to a large and splendid hall, wherein sat some enchanted princes whose rings he drew off their fingers. A sword and a loaf of bread were lying there, which he carried away. After this, he entered a chamber, in which was a beautiful maiden who rejoiced when she saw him, kissed him, and told him that he had set her free, and should have the whole of her kingdom, and that if he would return in a year their wedding should be celebrated; likewise she told him where the spring of the water of life was, and that he was to hasten and draw some of it before the clock struck twelve. Then he went onwards, and at last entered a room where there was a beautiful newly-made bed, and as he was very weary, he felt inclined to rest a little. So he lay down and fell asleep. When he awoke, it was striking a quarter to twelve. He sprang up in a fright, ran to the spring, drew some water in a cup which stood near, and hastened away. But just as he was passing through the iron door, the clock struck twelve, and the door fell to with such violence that it carried away a piece of his heel.

He, however, rejoicing at having obtained the water of life, went homewards, and again passed the dwarf. When the latter saw the sword and the loaf, he said: "With these you have won great wealth; with the sword you can slay whole armies, and the bread will never come to an end." But the prince would not go home to his father without his brothers, and said: "Dear dwarf, can you not tell me where my two brothers are? They went out before I did in search of the water of life, and have not returned." "They are imprisoned between two mountains," said the dwarf. "I have condemned them to stay there, because they were so haughty." Then the prince begged until the dwarf released them, but he warned him and said: "Beware of them, for they have bad hearts." When his brothers came, he rejoiced, and told them how things had gone with him, that he had found the water of life, and had brought a cupful away with him, and had rescued a beautiful princess, who was willing to wait a year for him, and then their wedding was to be celebrated, and he would obtain a great kingdom. After that they rode on together, and chanced upon a land where war and famine reigned, and the King already thought he must perish, for the scarcity was so great. Then the prince went to him and gave him the loaf, wherewith he fed and satisfied the whole of his kingdom, and then the prince gave him the sword also, wherewith he slew the hosts of his enemies, and could now live in rest and peace. The prince then took back his loaf and his sword, and the three brothers rode on. But after this they entered two more countries where war and famine reigned, and each time the prince gave his loaf and his sword to the Kings, and had now delivered three kingdoms, and after that they went on board a ship and sailed over the sea. During the passage, the two eldest conversed apart and said: "The youngest has found the water of life and not we, for that our father will give him the kingdom,—the kingdom which belongs to us, and he will rob us of all our fortune." They then began to seek revenge, and plotted with each other to destroy him. They waited until they found him fast asleep, then they poured the water of life out of the cup, and took it for themselves, but into the cup they poured salt sea-water.

Now therefore, when they arrived home, the youngest took his cup to the sick King in order that he might drink out of it, and be cured. But scarcely had he drunk a very little of the salt sea-water than he became still worse than before. And as he was lamenting over this, the two eldest brothers came, and accused the youngest of having intended to poison him, and said that they had brought him the true water of life, and handed it to him. He had scarcely tasted it, when he felt his sickness departing, and became strong and healthy as in the days of his youth. After that they both went to the youngest, mocked him, and said: "You certainly found the water of life, but you have had the pain, and we the gain; you should have been cleverer, and should have kept your eyes open. We took it from you whilst you were asleep at sea, and when a year is over, one of us will go and fetch the beautiful princess. But beware that you do not disclose aught[3] of this to our father; indeed he does not trust you, and if you say a single word, you shall lose your life into the bargain, but if you keep silent, you shall have it as a gift."

The old King was angry with his youngest son, and thought he had plotted against his life. So he summoned the court together, and had sentence pronounced upon his son, that he should be secretly shot. And once when the prince was riding forth to the chase, suspecting no evil, the King's huntsman was told to go with him, and when they were quite alone in the forest, the huntsman looked so sorrowful that the prince said to him: "Dear huntsman, what ails you?" The huntsman said: "I cannot tell you, and yet I ought." Then the prince said: "Say openly what it is, I will pardon you." "Alas!" said the huntsman, "I am to shoot you dead, the King has ordered me to do it." Then the prince was shocked, and said: "Dear huntsman, let me live; there, I give you my royal garments; give me your common ones in their stead." The huntsman said: "I will willingly do that, indeed I would not have been able to shoot you." Then they exchanged clothes, and the huntsman returned home, while the

---

3. **aught** any part; anything

prince went further into the forest. After a time three wagons of gold and precious stones came to the King for his youngest son, which were sent by the three Kings who had slain their enemies with the prince's sword, and maintained their people with his bread, and who wished to show their gratitude for it. The old King then thought: "Can my son have been innocent?" and said to his people: "Would that he were still alive, how it grieves me that I have suffered him to be killed!" "He still lives," said the huntsman, "I could not find it in my heart to carry out your command," and told the King how it had happened. Then a stone fell from the King's heart, and he had it proclaimed in every country that his son might return and be taken into favor again.

The princess, however, had a road made up to her palace which was quite bright and golden, and told her people that whosoever came riding straight along it to her, would be the right one and was to be admitted, and whoever rode by the side of it, was not the right one, and was not to be admitted. As the time was now close at hand, the eldest thought he would hasten to go to the King's daughter, and give himself out as her rescuer, and thus win her for his bride, and the kingdom to boot. Therefore he rode forth, and when he arrived in front of the palace, and saw the splendid golden road, he thought: "It would be a sin and a shame if I were to ride over that," and turned aside, and rode on the right side of it. But when he came to the door, the servants told him that he was not the right one, and was to go away again. Soon after this the second prince set out, and when he came to the golden road, and his horse had put one foot on it, he thought: "It would be a sin and a shame, a piece might be trodden off," and he turned aside and rode on the left side of it, and when he reached the door, the attendants told him he was not the right one, and he was to go away again. When at last the year had entirely expired, the third son likewise wished to ride out of the forest to his beloved, and with her forget his sorrows. So he set out and thought of her so incessantly, and wished to be with her so much, that he never noticed the golden road at all. So his horse rode onwards up the middle of it, and when he came to the door, it was opened and the princess received him with joy, and said he was her savior, and lord of the kingdom, and their wedding was celebrated with great rejoicing. When it was over she told him that his father invited him to come to him, and had forgiven him. So he rode thither, and told him everything; how his brothers had betrayed him, and how he had nevertheless kept silence. The old King wished to punish them, but they had put to sea, and never came back as long as they lived.

Joni Mitchell

The Circle Game

The stages of life are explained by the metaphorical carousel in this song by folk musician Joni Mitchell.

Yesterday a child came out to wonder
Caught a dragonfly inside a jar
Fearful when the sky was full of thunder
And tearful at the falling of a star
5   Then the child moved ten times round the seasons
Skated over ten clear frozen streams
Words like, when you're older, must appease[1] him
And promises of someday make his dreams
    And the seasons they go round and round
10   *And the painted ponies go up and down*
    We're captive on the carousel of time
    We can't return, we can only look behind
    From where we came
    And go round and round and round
15   *In the circle game*

Sixteen springs and sixteen summers gone new
Cartwheels turn to car wheels thru the town
And they tell him, Take your time, it won't be long now
Till you drag your feet to slow the circles down
20   *And the seasons they go round and round*
    And the painted ponies go up and down
    We're captive on the carousel of time
    We can't return, we can only look behind
    From where we came
25   *And go round and round and round*
    In the circle game

---

1. **appease** calm

So the years spin by and now the boy is twenty
Though his dreams have lost some grandeur² coming true
There'll be new dreams, maybe better dreams and plenty
30 Before the last revolving year is through.
    And the seasons they go round and round
    And the painted ponies go up and down
    We're captive on the carousel of time
    We can't return, we can only look behind
35 *From where we came*
    And go round and round and round
    In the circle game

---

2. **grandeur** magnificence

Washington Irving

from
Voyages and Discoveries of the Companions of Columbus

According to legend, the desire for everlasing life drove sixteenth-century explorer Juan Ponce de León to search for the fountain of youth.

Juan Ponce de Leon hears of a wonderful country and miraculous fountain.

Juan Ponce de Leon resigned the command of Porto Rico with tolerable[1] grace. The loss of one wild island and wild government was of little moment, when there was a new world to be shared out, where a bold soldier like himself, with sword and buckler,[2] might readily carve out new fortunes for himself. Beside, he had now amassed wealth to assist him in his plans, and, like many of the early discoverers, his brain was teeming[3] with the most romantic enterprises. He had conceived the idea that there was yet a third world to be discovered, and he hoped to be the first to reach its shores, and thus to secure a renown[4] equal to that of Columbus.

While cogitating[5] these things, and considering which way he

1. **tolerable** bearable
2. **buckler** small, round shield
3. **teeming** overflowing
4. **renown** fame
5. **cogitating** pondering; thinking carefully about

should strike forth in the unexplored regions around him, he met with some old Indians who gave him tidings[6] of a country which promised, not merely to satisfy the cravings[7] of his ambition,[8] but to realize the fondest dreams of the poets. They assured him that, far to the north, there existed a land abounding[9] in gold and in all manner of delights; but, above all, possessing a river of such wonderful virtue that whoever bathed in it would be restored to youth! They added, that in times past, before the arrival of the Spaniards, a large party of the natives of Cuba had departed northward in search of this happy land and this river of life, and, having never returned, it was concluded that they were flourishing[10] in renovated[11] youth, detained by the pleasures of that enchanting country.

Here was the dream of the Alchymist[12] realized! one had but to find this gifted land and revel in the enjoyment of boundless riches and perennial[13] youth! nay, some of the ancient Indians declared that it was not necessary to go so far in quest of these rejuvenating[14] waters, for that, in a certain island of the Bahama group, called Bimini, which lay far out in the ocean, there was a fountain possessing the same marvelous and inestimable[15] qualities.

Juan Ponce de Leon listened to these tales with fond credulity.[16] He was advancing in life, and the ordinary term of existence[17] seemed insufficient for his mighty plans. Could he but plunge into this marvelous fountain or gifted river, and come out with his battered, warworn body restored to the strength and freshness and suppleness[18] of youth, and his head still retaining the wisdom and knowledge of age,

---

6. **tidings** news; information
7. **cravings** intense or eager desires
8. **ambition** strong desire to succeed
9. **abounding** in great quantity; plentiful
10. **flourishing** thriving
11. **renovated** made like new
12. **Alchymist** *alchemist;* chemist in the Middle Ages whose intent was to turn common metals into gold
13. **perennial** enduring
14. **rejuvenating** making young again
15. **inestimable** very great
16. **credulity** willingness to believe
17. **term of existence** lifespan
18. **suppleness** flexibility

what enterprises might he not accomplish in the additional course[19] of vigorous years insured to him!

It may seem incredible, at the present day, that a man of years and experience could yield any faith to a story which resembles the wild fiction of an Arabian tale; but the wonders and novelties breaking upon the world in that age of discovery almost realised the illusions of fable, and the imaginations of the Spanish voyagers had become so heated that they were capable of any stretch of credulity.

So fully persuaded was the worthy old cavalier[20] of the existence of the region described to him, that he fitted out three ships at his own expense to prosecute[21] the discovery, nor had he any difficulty in finding adventurers in abundance ready to cruise with him in quest of this fairy-land.

Cruise of Juan Ponce de Leon in search of the Fountain of Youth.–(1512.)

It was on the third of March, 1512, that Juan Ponce sailed with his three ships from the Port of St. Germain in the island of Porto Rico. He kept for some distance along the coast of Hispaniola, and then, stretching away to the northward, made for the Bahama islands, and soon fell in with the first of the group. He was favoured with propitious[22] weather and tranquil[23] seas, and glided smoothly with wind and current along that verdant[24] archipelago,[25] visiting one island after another, until, on the fourteenth of the month, he arrived at Guanahani, or St. Salvador's, where Christopher Columbus had first put his foot on the shores of the new world. His inquiries for the island of Bimini were all in vain, and as to the fountain of youth, he may have drank of every fountain, and river, and lake, in the archipelago, even to the salt pools of Turk's island, without being a whit[26] the younger.

---

19. **course** duration
20. **cavalier** horseman
21. **prosecute** carry through; proceed with
22. **propitious** favorable
23. **tranquil** peaceful
24. **verdant** green with vegetation
25. **archipelago** large group of islands
26. **whit** bit

Still he was not discouraged; but, having repaired his ships, he again put to sea and shaped his course to the north-west. On Sunday, the 27th of March, he came in sight of what he supposed to be an island, but was prevented from landing by adverse weather. He continued hovering[27] about it for several days, buffeted[28] by the elements, until, in the night of the second of April, he succeeded in coming to anchor under the land in thirty degrees eight minutes of latitude. The whole country was in the fresh bloom of spring; the trees were gay with blossoms, and the fields covered with flowers; from which circumstance, as well as from having discovered it on Palm Sunday (Pascua Florida), he gave it the name of Florida, which it retains to the present day. The Indian name of the country was Cautio.

Juan Ponce landed, and took possession of the country in the name of the Castilian Sovereigns. He afterwards continued for several weeks ranging the coasts of this flowery land, and struggling against the gulf-stream and the various currents which sweep it. He doubled[29] Cape Cañaveral, and reconnoitered[30] the southern and eastern shores without suspecting that this was a part of Terra Firma.[31] In all his attempts to explore the country, he met with resolute[32] and implacable[33] hostility[34] on the part of the natives, who appeared to be a fierce and warlike race. He was disappointed also in his hopes of finding gold, nor did any of the rivers or fountains which he examined possess the rejuvenating virtue. Convinced, therefore, that this was not the promised land of Indian tradition, he turned his prow[35] homeward on the 14th of June, with the intention in the way of making one more attempt to find the island of Bimini.

In the outset of his return he discovered a group of islets abounding with sea-fowl and marine animals. On one of them his sailors,

---

27. **hovering** floating
28. **buffeted** battered; repeatedly attacked
29. **doubled** sailed around
30. **reconnoitered** surveyed; scouted out
31. **Terra Firma** solid ground; dry land
32. **resolute** firm
33. **implacable** unforgiving
34. **hostility** anger
35. **prow** forward part of a ship

in the course of a single night, caught one hundred and seventy turtles, and might have taken many more, had they been so inclined. They likewise took fourteen sea wolves, and killed a vast quantity of pelicans and other birds. To this group Juan Ponce gave the name of Tortugas, or turtles, which they still retain.

Proceeding in his cruise, he touched at another group of islets near the Lucayos, to which he gave the name of La Vieja, or the Old Woman group, because he found no inhabitant there but one old Indian woman. This ancient sybil he took on board his ship to give him information about the labyrinth[36] of islands into which he was entering, and perhaps he could not have had a more suitable guide in the eccentric[37] quest he was making. Notwithstanding her pilotage, however, he was exceedingly baffled and perplexed in his return voyage among the Bahama islands, for he was forcing his way as it were against the course of nature, and encountering the currents which sweep westward along these islands, and the trade-wind which accompanies them. For a long time he struggled with all kinds of difficulties and dangers; and was obliged to remain upwards of a month in one of the islands to repair the damages which his ship had suffered in a storm.

Disheartened at length by the perils and trials with which nature seemed to have beset the approach to Bimini, as to some fairy island in romance, he gave up the quest in person, and sent in his place a trusty captain, Juan Perez de Ortubia, who departed in one of the other ships, guided by the experienced old woman of the isles, and by another Indian. As to Juan Ponce, he made the best of his way back to Porto Rico, where he arrived infinitely poorer in purse and wrinkled in brow, by this cruise after inexhaustible riches and perpetual youth.

He had not been long in port when his trusty envoy,[38] Juan Perez, likewise arrived. Guided by the sage old woman, he had succeeded in finding the long-sought-for Bimini. He described it as being large, verdant, and covered with beautiful groves. There were crystal springs and limpid[39] streams in abundance, which kept the island in

---

36. labyrinth maze
37. eccentric uncommon; odd
38. envoy messenger
39. limpid clear

perpetual[40] verdure,[41] but none that could restore to an old man the vernal greenness[42] of his youth.

Thus ended the romantic expedition of Juan Ponce de Leon. Like many other pursuits of a chimera,[43] it terminated in the acquisition of a substantial good. Though he had failed in finding the fairy fountain of youth, he had discovered in place of it the important country of Florida.

---

40. **perpetual** constant
41. **verdure** fresh or flourishing condition
42. **vernal greenness** youthful immaturity
43. **chimera** dream

